Barbara Cartland's study of Clement Metternich, architect of the Congress of Vienna, and during his lifetime the saviour of Austria, concentrates on his personal rather than his political life. Born in Koblenz in 1773, Metternich was the second son of Count Franz Georg, a high official in the Imperial Court, and Countess Beatrice, an intelligent and beautiful woman. It was Beatrice who trained her son to grasp the importance of power. She taught him how to ingratiate himself with influential people, how to be hypocritical and at the same time shrewdly calculating. The result was a little boy who charmed all who met him – but a child with an over-developed sense of cunning...

Metternich's life was a series of amorous episodes. His mistresses included Constance de la Force, a high-born refugee from the French Revolution, Caroline Murat, Napoleon's sister, and Princess Katharina Bagration, mistress of the Tsar of Russia. And despite this philandering, Metternich inspired devoted love in his three wives...

Also by Barbara Cartland

Books of Love, Life and Health
THE YOUTH SECRET
THE MAGIC OF HONEY
THE MAGIC OF HONEY COOKBOOK
THE FASCINATING FORTIES
MEN ARE WONDERFUL
FOOD FOR LOVE
LOVE, LIFE AND SEX

Historical Biography
THE OUTRAGEOUS QUEEN
THE PRIVATE LIFE OF CHARLES II
THE SCANDALOUS LIFE OF KING CAROL
DIANE DE POITIERS

Romances
THE MAGNIFICENT MARRIAGE
THE KARMA OF LOVE
THE MASK OF LOVE
A SWORD TO THE HEART
BEWITCHED
THE IMPETUOUS DUCHESS
SHADOW OF SIN
GLITTERING LIGHTS
THE DEVIL IN LOVE
THE TEARS OF LOVE

and published by Corgi Books

Barbara Cartland

Metternich
The Passionate Diplomat

CORGI BOOKS
A DIVISION OF TRANSWORLD PUBLISHERS LTD

METTERNICH
A CORGI BOOK 0 552 10064 1

Originally published in Great Britain by
Hutchinson and Co. Ltd.

PRINTING HISTORY
Hutchinson edition published 1964
Corgi edition published 1976

Copyright © Barbara Cartland 1964

This low-priced Corgi Book has been completely reset in a
type face designed for easy reading, and was printed from
new plates. It contains the complete text of the
original hard-cover edition.

Conditions of sale
1: This book is sold subject to the condition that it
shall not, by way of trade *or otherwise*, be lent, re-sold,
hired out or otherwise *circulated* without the publisher's
prior consent in any form of binding or cover other than
that in which it is published *and without a similar
condition including this condition being imposed on
the subsequent purchaser.*
2: This book is sold subject to the Standard Conditions
of Sale of Net Books and may not be re-sold in the U.K.
below the net price fixed by the publishers for the book.

This book is set in 10/11pt. Times Roman

Corgi Books are published by Transworld Publishers Ltd.,
Century House, 61–63 Uxbridge Road,
Ealing, London, W.5.
Made and printed in Great Britain by
Hunt Barnard Printing Ltd., Aylesbury, Bucks.

Other Books by Barbara Cartland:

Romantic Novels, over 100, the most recently published being:

THE CASTLE OF FEAR
THE MASK OF LOVE
FIRE ON THE SNOW
A SWORD TO THE HEART
THE GLITTERING LIGHTS
THE KARMA OF LOVE
THE MAGNIFICENT MARRIAGE
BEWITCHED
THE IMPETUOUS DUCHESS
THE FRIGHTENED BRIDE

THE SHADOW OF SIN
THE FLAME IS LOVE
THE TEARS OF LOVE
A VERY NAUGHTY ANGEL
THE DEVIL IN LOVE
CALL OF THE HEART
LOVE IS INNOCENT
AS EAGLES FLY
SAY YES, SAMANTHA
A GAMBLE WITH HEARTS

Autobiographical and Biographical:
THE ISTHMUS YEARS 1919–1939
THE YEARS OF OPPORTUNITY 1939–1945
I SEARCH FOR RAINBOWS 1945–1966
WE DANCED ALL NIGHT 1919–1929
RONALD CARTLAND (WITH A FOREWORD BY SIR WINSTON CHURCHILL)
POLLY, MY WONDERFUL MOTHER

Historical:
BEWITCHING WOMEN
THE OUTRAGEOUS QUEEN (THE STORY OF QUEEN CHRISTINA OF SWEDEN)
THE SCANDALOUS LIFE OF KING CAROL
THE PRIVATE LIFE OF KING CHARLES II
THE PRIVATE LIFE OF ELIZABETH, EMPRESS OF RUSSIA
JOSEPHINE, EMPRESS OF FRANCE
DIANE DE POITIERS

Sociology:

YOU IN THE HOME
THE FASCINATING FORTIES
MARRIAGE FOR MODERNS
BE VIVID, BE VITAL
LOVE, LIFE AND SEX
VITAMINS FOR VITALITY
HUSBANDS AND WIVES
MEN ARE WONDERFUL

ETIQUETTE
THE MANY FACETS OF LOVE
SEX AND THE TEENAGER
THE BOOK OF CHARM
LIVING TOGETHER
THE YOUTH SECRET
THE MAGIC OF HONEY
FOOD FOR LOVE

THE MAGIC OF HONEY COOKBOOK
BARBARA CARTLAND'S HEALTH FOOD COOKERY BOOK
BARBARA CARTLAND'S BOOK OF BEAUTY AND HEALTH

Metternich

One

Eighteenth-century Koblenz was a city conscious of its timeless security. Nothing ever changed in its slow, sedate existence.

From the time when the Romans built a fort there, choosing the site because the Rhine and the Moselle merged below the steep banks, Koblenz had become lethargic in the assurance of its unassailability. Recurrent enemies looked at the great stone fortifications and barriers of water—and turned away.

For seven sleepy centuries the town had basked under the wise and beneficent rule of the Elector-Bishops of Trier. Through their intercession it appeared that God never forgot to favour the people of Koblenz. The citizens in their turn worshipped Him in the lovely ancient churches of St. Castor and St. Florin.

When the great bells of these churches rang out the people obeyed the summons to praise heaven or paused in their daily work to murmur a prayer of thanksgiving.

To support their spiritual contentment there was the comforting sight of secular invincibility just across the Rhine. The fantastic fortress of Ehrenbreitstein, perched on its 400-foot-high rock, was called by the strangers who eyed its rich area with greedy hopes 'the Gibraltar of the Rhine'.

To the people of Koblenz the term was meaningless. Few troubled themselves with places beyond their own dear land, and those whose education told them of other strategically important zones would have, on seeing Gibraltar, dubbed it 'the Ehrenbreitstein of the Mediterranean'.

It was in this town that a child was born on May 15th,

1773, whose whole life was to be devoted to the veneration of tradition and the upholding of the *status quo*.

The baby came into a world rumbling with the first signs of new political patterns. Away to the East, powerful nations had begun the policy of temporarily settling their major differences while they devoured a helpless neighbour. Poland had recently been shared out among Austria, Russia and Prussia—three enemies momentarily placid and content after a highly satisfying feast.

Away to the West, the settlers in the New World were flexing their muscles and unleashing the spirit of freedom. A deceptively small incident had occurred in Boston Harbour when the colonists made a gesture against the hated tea tax.

Of even greater significance was the fact that the world was becoming bigger. Cook had come back with his amazing stories of Polynesia, of the vast continent which was Australia, of the immensity of the Pacific.

The people of Koblenz were not interested in the great restless world beyond their city walls. Their blindness would, in time, bring about their downfall. But their obstinate worship of tradition was to motivate the life of the new-born baby who would go into history as their greatest son—yet as a son who, in the final analysis, failed.

Clement Wenceslas Nepomuk Lothar was born in the shabby Metternich Hof, one of the most grandiose of all the once beautiful residences in the city.

It was a house built in the middle ages—and behind its lovely facade there was decay and discomfort. Its day of glory had in fact long passed. Only the prestige of its history remained.

The Metternichs—preoccupied as every other family in the town, from the humblest craftsman to the Elector-Bishop himself, with matters of ancestry—boasted that the family was as old as the Christian era.

As is inevitably the case, incidents which at the time had insinuated illicit behaviour or a decided fall from grace, had with the passage of time become embellished with magnificence.

In the case of the Metternich family the oft-told story was that the great Charlemagne himself had relied for his triumphs on his trusted friend and comrade in arms, the Chevalier Metter.

There was jealousy among the courtiers at the Chevalier's privileged position. Finally they had forced upon a priest the unpleasant duty of informing the Emperor that Metter had presumed on his intimate relationship with the Imperial household by enjoying the favours of the Empress while Charlemagne was absent.

Charlemagne, not unduly careful about his own amorous exploits, listened to the tale with disbelief and even amusement. Possibly he considered that no Knight would have risked his neck for a few minutes' pleasure in forbidden territory; perhaps he preferred to turn a blind eye to the fault of a friend who was of enormous value to him in the business of extending and protecting the Holy Roman Empire.

Whatever the reason, the Emperor was reputed to have reproved the priest with the comment:

'Metter to betray me? Of all men, you cite Metter? *Nicht!*'

It was, of course, a typically legendary explanation of a name whose real origin was submerged in the sands of time.

But the story achieved its purpose; for it pointed out that when Europe was in the making there had been a warrior Knight with the family name—and a man, to boot, who had been the trusted intimate of the greatest Emperor of the Christian era. A Knight who had, in fact, put his blood into the Royal line through an illicit amour.

There was no reason why this explanation of the ancient origin of the Metternichs should not have been perfectly true, because by the mediaeval era, when records became reasonably plentiful and reliable, there were documents and memorial stones in the churches of Koblenz (St. Castor had been consecrated in the ninth century) proving a distinguished and unblemished line at least as far back as the year A.D. 1000.

These records gave every reason for pride. Many of the Metternichs had died early in life, falling in battle against their master's enemies. Three had been raised to princedoms and generation after generation had held important posts in the courts of German Dukes and Princelings.

They had always been ready to place their wealth and their lives at the disposal of those they considered by birth and divine right were their superiors. The result had been more than glory and titles. Grateful overlords had rewarded the Metternich family with splendid estates. Acre upon acre in the fertile countryside of the Rhineland belonged to them.

By the time little Clement was born this glory no longer scintillated. Lethargy and pomposity had dulled the brilliance of the Metternich character.

Clement's father, Count Franz Georg von Metternich-Winneburg, was only twenty-seven but he had the appearance of a man in middle age and the mental agility of a senescent greybeard. His birth automatically made him a person of some political importance. He was Chamberlain to the Archbishop of Mainz and a high official in the Imperial Court. Neither post entailed much responsibility: they were merely the means of reaching greater power.

Early in his career Count Franz Georg had decided that the machinations of politics and diplomacy were too much for him, and he had publicly stated that he despised modern ruthlessness.

'Everything will work out one way or another like everything else,' was his favourite and characteristically stupid comment when confronted by a dilemma. He might have found a comfortable niche in the Imperial direction of Central Europe if he had been disposed to exert himself sufficiently. But he was chronically lazy, both mentally and physically.

When he was quite young the Count had decided to ignore the important in favour of the trivial. In the realm of the latter he was able to claim expertness. No one knew more about formalized etiquette; no Hof in all the Empire was conducted with such rigid ritual. No servant, even in the Imperial Court itself, was clothed in such gorgeous livery.

No self-examination of the essential futility of his life could have disturbed Count Franz Georg. He was a happy man. For this eminently desirable state of affairs he undoubtedly would have ascribed his own design for living. In actual fact the even tenor of his days was as much due to his clever and charming wife as his own policy of lethargy.

Countess Beatrice was a highly intelligent and very lovely woman. Theirs was hardly a love match, for the union had been authorized, and therefore planned, by the Empress Maria Theresa.

She had the pretty, headstrong child Marie-Beatrice de Kagenegg as a protégée; she had the dull but socially important Franz Georg hanging around the Court, womanizing and making a nuisance of himself. A marriage appeared an ideal way of giving the girl a role worthy of her energy and of getting the Count back to his estates on the Rhine where he could devote himself to breeding yet another generation of Metternichs.

The coldly planned marriage turned out remarkably well. The young husband admired the way his wife took over the burden of detail in running the household and was constantly grateful for her quick and sensible solutions of such problems as even he could not avoid in his political career.

Whatever frustrations Beatrice felt once she had been whisked away to the comparative savagery of life on the banks of the Rhine, as compared with the exotic conditions beside the Danube, she contrived to conceal them.

She would have had reason to lapse into despair. Not only did her husband quickly become fat and lethargic, but the first child he gave her was as characterless as he was himself.

Their daughter Pauline was awkward in body and stupid in mind. Bitterly disappointed, Countess Beatrice prayed at subsequent confinements for a baby fashioned more in her own image. She was to have another disappointment in her son Pepe who was obstinate and lazy.

But these two were a minor price to pay for the bounteous blessings that came with the birth of Clement. He was, even as a tiny baby, uncannily like his mother—the same oval face, high forehead, finely moulded features and large expressive eyes.

Countess Beatrice doted on her second son. She dreamed of a great future for him, and took action to ensure those dreams should have a chance of coming true.

Clement's wit and charm, his light touch in conversation, his brilliant approach to new ideas, his dexterous adaptability to circumstance, his fluent knowledge of French all stemmed from these first lessons with his mother.

But some of the things he learned in her boudoir were hardly of the kind described as morally uplifting.

Countess Beatrice was fashioning her son's mind to grasp power. Until it was obtained he would, she taught him, have to ingratiate himself with those who had influence. Hypocrisy, the white lie, the deceptive comment and the shrewd calculation of ways and means were all ingrained in his mind at those lessons. The result was a little boy who charmed all who met him—but a child with a sense of cunning so precocious that few recognized it for what it was.

'In Germany,' his mother wrote to him, 'you must admire German music, and French music when in France, and the same applies to most things.'

At seventeen the Countess described Clement as 'the most successful messenger I know'.

Every detail of young Clement's education was personally supervised by the Countess, and as a result was far more comprehensive than his father had ever envisaged.

The Countess was no scatterbrained lady of the Court, but an ambitious and intelligent woman who had seen in Maria Theresa the power that even a woman could have when well educated. It was all very bewildering to her husband, whose idea of instruction for his son was to have clergy and obsequious clerks describe the importance of the Rhine Palatinate in general and the Metternich family in particular.

He did, however, give his son some advice which he himself had always found most helpful.

'Comport yourself seemly,' he said, 'be helpful to all men and never underestimate old women whose gossip can make or unmake a young man's career more than you might suppose. Be flexible, be obliging, that's most important.'

Count Franz Georg was intimidated by his son's early grasp of Imperial affairs, but true to his easy-going nature preferred to leave things to his wife. Yet the reticent but persistent activities of the Countess sometimes forced the Count to bestir himself more than he liked. His appointment as Imperial Ambassador to the Courts of the Rhineland indicated that the Empress had not forgotten her protégée, while Beatrice in her turn saw to it that this post was not regarded as a sinecure.

It meant considerable travelling for the Count, which was bad enough; worse was the need to understand the political situation. There was, however, one great compensation. An Ambassador's dress was expected to be commensurate with the magnificence of the Empire he represented.

In this, at least, Count Franz Georg was outstanding. He was rarely seen without a magnificently embroidered waistcoat, ornate and valuable buttons, silk breeches fastened with silver buckles over silk stockings, a mass of foamy lace at his neck and wrists, and an overpowering wig. Obese and short as he was, the effect was not without its impressiveness.

What was more, the Emperor Francis appreciated a sportsman who was apparently prepared nearly to ruin himself in order to dazzle the crowd at a coronation or on other occasions by the gorgeous brilliance of his liveries 'scarlet velvet, trimmed with heavy gold braid'.

Treilhard when he met the Count at the Congress of Rastadt described him as 'cold, arrogant, impertinent, on occasion a stickler for convention, endowed with little understanding and consequently obstinate as a mule', while two Jacobin delegates to the same Congress noted that the Minister was 'starchy, over-ceremonious, unintelligent and obstinate'.

Koblenz was ruled by an Archbishop. Religion imposed a secular and spiritual discipline on every citizen, high or low born. Count Franz Georg, though not a particularly religious man, accepted the situation as the only possible one, mainly because church rule had always existed and any change would be for the worse.

There was also ample evidence from the power and wealth of the Metternich family that the alliance between a warrior family and the church hierarchy had in the past worked excellently for both parties.

The Countess was, of course, Catholic, but privately she believed that the Church should serve not dominate in worldly matters.

The result was that Clement was taught by tutors who were widely read in works frowned upon by the Papacy—the philosophies of men in England, France and Scandinavia who were breaking through the walls of bigotry. There was even a Protestant teacher among the men brought to the rambling old house at Koblenz.

At fifteen Clement matriculated. His father believed that the boy would automatically enter one of the German universities. He was, in fact, so convinced of the inevitability of this final stage of his son's education that he never mentioned the matter. It was therefore to his mystification, and even alarm, that he learned that the Countess had completed arrangements for Clement to enter the University of Strasbourg.

Strasbourg was at the time the most enlightened seat of learning in the world—and for that very reason highly suspect to men of the old guard like Count Franz Georg.

For one thing the town was outside the confines of the Empire; worse, it was full of radicals on the professional staff. An ex-monk named Johann Simon had gained both notoriety and fame as a devotee of the dangerous philosophies of Rousseau and Voltaire. Professors of history proclaimed the glory of the revolution which had brought freedom to the colonists of America; plenty looked forward to revolution in France and in the rest of Europe.

For a boy of sixteen Strasbourg in 1788 offered almost irresistible influences towards radicalism. It was proof that he had inherited some of his father's character as well as his mother's brains that Clement Metternich dutifully attended the lectures of the radical professors but reserved his loyalties for the German-born teachers who maintained the conservative traditions.

In making this decision he settled the pattern of his life. At Strasbourg in those months on the eve of the French Revolution it was not merely a case of making a private decision on political ideologies; one had to proclaim one's views and join one side or the other in the violent arguments which interminably prevailed among the students.

That Clement Metternich chose wisely was shown later when Nicholas Vogt, his teacher in Mainz, spoke to him in words he never forgot:

'Your intelligence and your heart,' Vogt said, 'are well set in the right way; persevere also in active life; the lessons of history will be your guide. Long as your career may be you will not see the end of the conflagration that is consuming a great State at our doors. If you do not wish to incur reproach, never leave the right road. You will see supposedly great men pass you in the race. Let them be and do not quit your intended path. You will catch them up again, if only because you will come across them as they retrace their steps.'

It was the practice for young men of noble blood at the University to have a guardian. In the case of Clement his mentor was a Bavarian, Prince Max von Zweibrucken, Colonel of the Royal Alsatian Dragoons, the unit which manned the Strasbourg defences.

The Dragoons were in effect the Colonel's private army; he owned the men; their arms and their equipment. For his protégé, the wealth and influence of Prince Max meant a life of luxury.

It was in this environment that Clement first enjoyed social pleasures of a kind quite foreign to the heavy and serious friends and relatives in his native town.

With the rumblings of the French Revolution growing into a thunderous storm of disaster for the aristocracy of France, Strasbourg rapidly filled with refugees. Most of them believed optimistically their visit to be a brief interruption of their accustomed life, and that after a few weeks order would be restored and they would be back in Paris and Versailles.

In the meanwhile there was no reason why the stay in the old Alsatian city should not be made as amusing as possible. The refugees had brought money and valuables with them. They made it possible to enjoy a round of entertainment which both served to banish the boredom of life in a strange and rather sedate provincial town and to suppress the nagging fear that the France they knew was, despite every protestation to the contrary, disappearing for ever.

Among the refugees was one who everyone regarded as one of the loveliest young women in France. Marie-Constance was the daughter of the Marquis de Saville, Keeper of the Seals.

She had been married at the age of sixteen to the Duc de Caumont la Force. The union was contrived as being mutually beneficial. The Duc was brother of the mistress of the Comte de France, the King's brother. Constance was heiress to a vast fortune and the daughter of a man with enormous influence; she was, in addition, very beautiful.

'She dazzled,' said the Marquis de Bouillé in his memoirs, 'the first flush and brilliance of youth combined with the seductive qualities of a supremely beautiful woman.'

For once the usual description of beauty in any young woman of aristocratic birth and political importance was supported by facts. Portraits of Constance show a tall, beautifully moulded girl with the carriage of an athlete, unusual for her sex in that age. Her face had a magnetic quality, partly due to her large, wide-apart eyes below a rounded brow. Her mouth was generous with a pouting lower lip hinting at exuberant sexuality. The perfect oval of her chin set off her intriguing features to perfection.

'No painter could have wished a better model for Hebe or a Psyche,' the Marquis continues. 'Such qualities were fated to conquer all comers! How indeed could a man resist them when added to all this the lady was a bit of a coquette—the more effective in that she operated under a guise of ingenuousness, one might almost say of innocence.'

Constance was eighteen when she was living in Strasbourg. Her husband was stationed at Nancy. Until the Revolution made absence from duty impossible he was able to visit his wife regularly. But these visits were not sufficiently frequent to placate Constance. She felt bored and frustrated. The Duc unwisely sought to help her banish her restlessness by giving her still more money so that she could enjoy herself.

The focal point of the refugees' existence in Strasbourg was the Inn of the Three Golden Crowns. Here gambling tables had been set up and the largest room decorated and furnished as a dancing salon. The tavern was a large one, and there was a series of dining rooms ranging from those big enough for a couple of dozen guests to discreet little converted bedrooms for more intimate occasions.

Clement was taken by his guardian to a social event at the inn. It was not intended he should stay long; it was really in the nature of a young German aristocrat paying formal respects to a few French people his guardian considered it would be correct for him to meet.

The gaiety and splendour of the crowd on what was an ordinary evening mesmerized the young student. For the Inn of the Three Golden Crowns was Paris, glittering in all its brilliance against the simple background of intellectual Strasbourg. The uniforms and the gowns were what the guests would have worn at the Palais Royale. Jewels worth a king's ransom accentuated the deep *décolleté* of the elaborate and seductive gowns, powdered hair and French scent which made the women move in an aura of fragrance, and were something which Clement had never encountered before.

Never gauche or at a loss for the appropriate gesture and word of conventional politeness, it was clear to anyone watching him that he was for the moment tongue-tied.

One person who saw his disquiet was Constance de la Force, sitting bored and restless as she tried to win at the gambling tables the piles of *Louis d'or* that meant nothing if she did acquire them. The buttons of her dress were all of rubies and diamonds and she wore a fortune around her neck and on her wrists. There was nothing she wanted—nothing, she had told herself often enough—but the sight of this slim, handsome blue-eyed young man among people who for the most part were middle-aged intrigued her.

She rose from the table and asked who the stranger was. On being told that he was a young Count from Koblenz, the protégé of Prince Max, she immediately insisted that she should make his acquaintance.

'Make up a small party for dinner tomorrow night,' she said imperiously to the Marquis de Bouillé. 'Include the boy; he looks as if he's lonely and out of his depth. One never knows: a family of the right kind across the Rhine may be useful friends if . . .'

The Marquis knew what she meant. More and more the refugees in Strasbourg were looking across the borders of France for their next escape route. But he was amused as well. Constance was not the kind to show fear. He guessed the real motive for her demand was to further a passing interest.

'I could ill defend myself,' the Marquis confessed in his diary, 'from a seduction which flattering pride and natural inclination became the more pungent by the very fact that I was not the sole recipient of the lady's favours.'

Amused if piqued at being involved in a new intrigue, the Marquis duly arranged the dinner party of half a dozen guests for the following evening. A servant was waiting to leave the invitations on his friends next morning when Constance was announced.

'I want,' she said with a smile, 'to alter my request. Have you chosen close friends—other than the boy, of course—who will not be offended if you belatedly and suddenly cancel your invitation?'

The Marquis laughed.

'Knowing your mind, Madame, I have thought of that. Look!'

He handed her the envelopes.

'I know them well,' he continued. 'They will all have half a dozen other invitations, so they will not mind in the least if I apologize this afternoon for having made a mistake.'

'Splendid,' Constance smiled. 'You are a good friend.' She leaned forward and kissed his cheek. 'The Prince will, of course, confirm who the other guests are likely to be before he allows this young Count to accept.'

She glanced over the addresses.

'A priest, a Princess, a retired General and his wife, myself,' she murmured. 'That is perfect! His Highness is bound to approve.'

At midday Clement was penning his grateful acceptance under the tutelage of his guardian. By late afternoon all acceptances had been delivered, and an hour later all the guests except Constance and Clement had been put off.

At first the dinner was not a success. Despite Constance's efforts, Clement remained silent and awkward. Even the champagne did not loosen his tongue. It was not that he was shy but worried if he had offended convention in staying when the other guests had failed to arrive.

He had not known what to do, fearing to insult his companion if he suggested that they depart without dinner and dreading that he would compromise her if he remained. The latter seemed the inevitable disaster when he found himself ushered into a private room.

Outside there was the gambling salon with its green *boiseries* and golden *baquettes*. Here there was quiet save for the distant music of violins. Clement felt as if he and this lovely woman were alone in an oasis where time had ceased to matter.

He was conscious of her full red lips, of the cleft between her breasts as she bent forward to speak to him, of the strange expression in her eyes which fascinated yet frightened him.

He drank to her in a long-stemmed champagne glass and it seemed as if she exuded some strange magnetism which brought the blood pounding into his veins. Why should he be worried and afraid?

The refugees from France could show him how to live. The mob might be howling through the streets of Paris but still they danced and laughed.

'*Vive la vie!*' was their slogan. '*Vive la jeunesse!*'

Before the meal was over Constance fell silent.

'I have a headache,' she complained. 'I fear I must ask you to escort me home.'

Her sedan chair was brought to the door of the inn. A few people glanced amusedly at the couple leaving so early: it meant only one thing at the Three Golden Crowns.

Clement said he would be honoured if he could walk alongside the chair, but from the shadows of the interior Constance made a protest.

'There is room for two in here,' she said. 'We are both slender enough for the seat. Come . . .'

A gloved hand appeared through the curtain and felt for his arm. Clement obeyed the gesture.

At the house a flunkey opened the door, closed it behind them, and at a murmured order from Constance disappeared. Candles flickered at intervals up the stairs and along the hallway. Constance led Clement by the hand, pausing at the door of her boudoir, which he opened. She moved forward, her silk skirts rustling over the carpeted floor. Clement stood, awkward and embarrassed, on the threshold.

'But come in,' she commanded. 'I will not keep you long. There is wine on the table by the fire.'

She vanished through the open door on the far side of the room. Clement watched her go, and then hastily lowered his gaze. A four-poster, imposing and inviting, its draperies drawn back, stood in the centre of the room.

Constance was back with him in a matter of minutes. She was wearing only a white batiste wrapper edged with Valenciennes lace. It fluttered around her, but her nudity beneath it was all too obvious. Her incredibly small feet were in white satin slippers and with the ghost of a smile she moved almost silently towards Clement.

He was trembling as he rose from the chair on which he had been sitting. The robe fell away from her exquisite pointed breasts leaving them framed in the billowing white lace.

Gently, very gently, she put her arms around him and kissed him on the mouth, and his arms went round her, feeling the soft warmth of her excited young body. . . .

It was almost dawn when Clement crept down the stairs. The same flunkey who had let them in appeared from the shadows in the hall and bowed respectfully as he opened the door. Clement walked from the house and through the streets to his own lodgings.

The light was just touching the roof-tops, and the peasants were coming into the town from the countryside, their carts piled high with vegetables, eggs and chickens.

In the Güttenbergplatz the candlelight still shimmered through the curtains of the Inn of the Three Golden Crowns. Guests were waiting on the steps for their carriages and their sedan chairs. Their laughter seemed hollow on the clear, cool morning air.

Clement drew back his head proudly—last night he had been a boy, this morning he was a man.

A youth's first introduction to sexual love in the arms of an older and experienced woman is usual enough to be almost banal. Clement Metternich's affair with Constance de la Force was of the standard pattern, for even if she was only a year or so his senior she was married and sophisticated.

But the fact that she was young enough to be envisaged as a mate, thus eradicating the influence of an Oedipus complex, profoundly affected Metternich's life for ever.

His attitude to women, and indirectly to the adversities and allies he had in his spectacular career, was moulded by that night in Strasbourg.

He ascribed to the affair an idealism and perfection which were probably not really endorsed by Constance, though Metternich's subsequent career might have helped her to embellish the memory with more profundity than was justified.

He never forgot the rapturous magic of that night. Later he was to write:

'I loved her with all the enthusiasm of youth, and she loved me with all the simplicity of her heart. We both desired what in fact we never sought: I lived only for her and for my studies. She had nothing to do except to love me.'

Two

To glamorize the actual seduction contrived by Constance as anything more than a passing amusement where she was concerned or to make it more than a callow infatuation for Clement would be absurd.

Nevertheless, as is so often the case when passions are ignited, both had started a fire which burned brighter than she expected or he had ever dreamed was possible.

Clement obtained from the experience the knowledge that he was attractive to women—always a matter of enormous satisfaction to a male adolescent with all the forebodings and fears of unformed emotional immaturity.

He was to write many years later:

'I made the acquaintance at this time of a young woman of my age, an exquisite creature full of charm, good taste and wit. She belonged to one of the great families of France. This relationship lasted more than three years and had for me the invaluable advantage of turning me away from the indiscretions of bad taste that are common at that age.'

He also discovered that the rigid formalism of love among men and women of his class and environment was a disguise of the real facts. He knew, of course, that aristocrats like his father seduced serving maids and resorted to prostitutes. But by the standards of his class-conscious upbringing these were only lowly women who had nothing but animal passions.

Now he realized that sexual desire could be a motive for love between aristocratic equals just as much as the economic or social benefits in marriage. This was one truth which his mother, with her tolerant and realistic policy on education, had ignored. She had never known passion.

The sheer physical ecstasy of love-making, the ease with which it could be practised, and the absence of world-shattering repercussions, amazed and intrigued Clement.

He had been brought up as a strict Catholic. At the University he instinctively made friends with the reactionary and devout teachers no matter how much his keen and enquiring brain delighted in the fresh outlook of the humanists and the radicals. In committing adultery he might well have been tortured by a sense of sin but for one thing.

His first woman became his ideal woman. Time added beauty to the memory; sporadic renewals of the affair only confirmed his belief in Constance's perfection. For the rest of his life Clement was probably always seeking the perfection, the beauty and the ecstasy of that first night of love. Of course, he never found it again. But he never gave up looking for it, not even in advanced age.

And for Constance, cynical, restless and sybaritic as she was, the hour of pleasure she had so carelessly contrived to relieve the boredom of her life took on some of the magic with which Clement endowed it.

For a fleeting moment she, too, climbed the heights of passion, and found a passion that was almost divine.

Their first meeting took place shortly before Clement was due to leave for Mainz where he would continue his studies, specializing in law. The town was as packed with French aristocrats as Strasbourg, and no suspicion was created in the Duc de la Force's mind when his wife told him that she wished to move to Mainz.

The growing dangers of the Revolution made such a change reasonable, and soon Constance was seeing her young lover again. This time they openly admitted their friendship.

Clement was rapidly growing up. Either from Constance's own lips, or from mutual friends, he learned that he was not the lady's sole lover. Whatever shock such information may have aroused in his heart, he made no jealous scenes.

The Marquis de Bouillé, writing of this in his diary, said:

'This obligation to share her solicitude, this twin distraction, far from putting any painful rivalry between myself and Metternich had established a kind of intimacy between us, almost a friendship. The coincidence of our affection appears to have drawn us together rather than the reverse and our hearts overflowed in agreeable communication on our frequent walks (invariably together) towards Madame's house in that lovely alley of the Rhine.'

This was indeed a training in cynicism and dissimulation for the future diplomat!

But, like all lovers, Clement and Constance were content to live in the present and forget everything else, rivals as well as the world outside.

As Clement wrote later:

'When we were together we gave each other assurances of love and the future stretched such a long way before our eyes that we put off the sequel to so much love until a more opportune moment.'

The pleasant years at Mainz ended abruptly when Count Franz Georg ordered Clement to leave immediately for Frankfurt. The short reign of Leopold II had ended, and his son Francis was to be crowned.

Clement, as the elder son of one of the oldest families in Westphalia, had been commanded to present the Counts of the Rhineland to the new Emperor. His parents had already left for the city.

In the days prior to the Coronation Clement formed a friendship which was to be of vital importance to his career—and to the Europe of the approaching nineteenth century. The new Emperor was only four years older than Clement. The two young men were attracted to one another, and Francis was greatly impressed with his companion's vivid description of conditions in Strasbourg, by his reports of first-hand accounts by refugees of events in Paris and by his assessment of the rumblings of revolution in Strasbourg itself.

In his turn Clement was flattered by the new Emperor's friendly attitude, and impressed by his obvious and unaffected devotion of the Empire.

In 1792 they had, although neither of them knew it, come to the end of an era. In Paris anarchy reigned; the nobility of France were tramping into exile; at the Tuileries there was agony of mind, humiliation and depression, while all established forms of Government had fallen.

In Frankfurt illuminations, processions and magnificent *fiesta* kept before everyone's mind the splendour of the Coronation.

No one could have failed to be stirred, least of all Clement, educated from birth in his own family's historical importance, as the crown worn by Charlemagne was being placed on the head of the new ruler of the Holy Roman Empire.

The Emperor turned to face the Knights in their magnificent robes of purple and red, green trimmed with ermine, and the nobles in their glittering coronets and decorations. They unsheathed their swords in salutation and a thunderous cry roared through the cathedral.

'*Vivat! Vivat! Vivat Imperator Noster!*'

The new reign brought great changes for the Metternich family. Clement's father was appointed Minister in the Austrian Netherlands, a post of importance in view of the country's proximity to revolutionary France. The post was a reward for services rendered during the Coronation but was quite beyond the capabilities of a man like Count Franz Georg Metternich.

In a country seething with unrest he continued to devote himself to the nicer points of precedence and the design of Court dress. The Imperial Government could not understand how letters to him appeared to get lost on the way or were at least hopelessly delayed. Finally it was discovered that the sight of a cover with the Imperial seal so worried their Netherlands Minister that he took the easy way out of losing the letter or leaving it unopened for days on end.

The presence of the elder Metternich in the Netherlands gave his son the opportunity of widening his interests. This was largely at the behest of the Crown Prince of Prussia (later Frederick William II), who was commanding the Prussian Army, in camp two or three miles from the Metternich house at Koblenz.

The Prince advised Clement to continue with his studies, taking advantage of tuition outside his own country by attending the University of Brussels and simultaneously giving some much needed assistance to his father.

In fact, the obvious incompetence of the elder Metternich and the recurrent political crises of the time meant that attendance at the University was constantly interrupted.

All through the winter of 1793-4 Metternich was travelling with letters and messages from the Netherlands to the Austrian Army.

Sometimes he was close to the scene of hostilities. He observed the siege of Valenciennes, helping to receive prisoners and expelled diplomats during the action of the French troops invading the Netherlands. And he was particularly horrified when the news of the execution of Marie Antoinette arrived.

Infuriated by the inefficiency of Metternich senior, and impressed by the way his young son was doing his best to take over such duties as he could, the Austrian authorities suggested to the Emperor that Clement be given an official post. He was thereupon made Minister Plenipotentiary of the Emperor at The Hague, and it was in this office that he accompanied the Chief Treasurer of the Netherlands Government on a special mission to England.

The English Ambassador's messages from Vienna reported that the young man, while a member of an unimportant Rhenish family, was an intimate of the new Emperor, and this paved the way for Clement to be welcomed at the Court of St. James's with greater friendliness than his status or his age warranted.

George III had recovered from a period of insanity, and the reaction had been a renewed nation-wide regard for the King, which the outbreak of the French Revolution enhanced.

Clement arrived in England holding the universal belief of Europeans that the King of England represented the nucleus of opposition to France, and was the upholder of the policies which the revolutionaries sought to destroy.

For this reason the young German approached the London scene with a feeling of veneration, and he was eager to meet the Ministers whose duty it was to carry out the monarch's policies.

His political acumen was quickly recognized, and he was welcomed into the homes of men like Pitt, Fox, Sheridan, Grey and, most important, Burke. They all received him 'with great affability'.

But the social world of England was focussed entirely on the Prince of Wales, the First Gentleman of Europe, who was hardly on speaking terms with his father because of the profligacy of his life, and his political outlook. The Prince was still officially single, although all his friends and a goodly part of the country knew of his long 'liaison' with Mrs. Fitzherbert, so proper and ladylike in her behaviour that she seemed more like a wife than a mistress.

Not unwillingly Clement was drawn away from the serious and austere circles round the King into the extravagances and excesses of the world of fashion headed by the Prince.

He was tutored by Beau Brummell in the finer points of dress and manners, and enjoyed the intimacies of the courtesans and ladies of fashion—hardly distinguishable by any difference in their morals—who were only too anxious to entertain this charming young man from Europe.

From the Admiral's flagship he watched a review of the Grand Fleet, just off the Isle of Wight.

'No more beautiful sight could ever meet the eye,' he said of the 400 sailing vessels.

It was a pleasant, perhaps too pleasant, six months. Subsequent activities showed that Clement was absorbing knowledge of the English mentality and making a careful estimate of the country's military power and international outlook, as well as enjoying himself.

The English phase, provided more or less as a holiday at the end of his studies and to fill the interval while the family problems solved themselves, was of inestimable value. By the time he returned home in October 1794 Clement had changed from a youth to an accomplished, self-reliant man of twenty-one.

He went straight to Vienna, where his father, without an official post and without his family home, was trying to maintain his position among the vast number of hangers-on who surrounded the Viennese Court. Count Franz Georg was perfectly content to jog along, living on past glories and hoping that another sinecure would in time be found for him.

Countess Beatrice, however, had gone to Vienna with only one idea: to further her son's career. Womanlike, the first step seemed to her to be the arrangement of a propitious marriage. As soon as Clement arrived he was told of her plans. Mother and son thought alike and when they aimed at anything they aimed high. Beatrice was offering him both money and influence.

'I am hoping you will marry into the Kaunitz family,' she said as soon as they were alone, and saw by the sudden widening of his eyes that he was surprised.

Princess Eleonore von Kaunitz was a girl anyone in the Empire would have been glad to marry. Twenty years old, she was reasonably attractive. As the only grand-daughter of the recently dead Chancellor who had been both Maria Theresa's greatest friend and the most powerful diplomat of his day in Central Europe, she was illustrious and rich.

Suitors from the greatest families in Austria had sought her hand and only the family mourning for her grandfather and her own capricious lack of interest in them had prevented her being married off before Clement came on the scene.

That one of the most marriageable young women in the Empire finally bestowed her hand and her fortune on Clement Metternich was entirely due to the efforts of his mother.

She was deeply worried at the eclipse of the family fame and fortune. Her husband's record in the Netherlands had been disastrous. The Emperor himself had complained about conditions he found when he visited the country, and perhaps his courteous observation that he believed his Minister's inefficiency was 'at least based on good intentions' was the cruellest cut of all. All Vienna was avidly repeating the Emperor's view that Count Franz Georg was not a villain but a fool.

Not only had the French swept into the Netherlands and snapped them up with a minimum of trouble but the troops had poured across the Rhine and most of the Metternich lands had been occupied. All the timeless security of name, land and position had disappeared in a matter of days.

Count Franz Georg had lost three and a half square German miles of land, 6,200 'vassals' and 50,000 florins of income. Clement realized in this that everything he held dear was being menaced—privilege, money, social standing, in fact the whole foundation of his life. It was during his sojourn in the Netherlands that he had first seen himself predestined as a 'guardian of that social order' which the enemy had set out to destroy.

In August 1794 Clement Metternich had published an anonymous tract 'on the necessity of arming all populations adjoining the French frontiers'.

'The French Revolution,' he wrote, 'has reached a pitch where it menaces the whole of Europe . . . the object of these modern barbarians is to break with all social convention, to destroy accepted principles and confiscate property. . . . Unite, the brigand hordes will flee before your face; reputable men of all nations will flock up to your banners. Europe will owe you her preservation and future generations their peace.'

The life-long relentless enemy of the revolution, the Chancellor-to-be and the future inventor of the Metternich 'system', had spoken for the first time.

Although Count Franz Georg had proceeded to Vienna on the pretext of consultation on the crisis in Imperial affairs he was in reality little more than a penniless refugee. His attempts to maintain his pomposity either annoyed or merely amused the haughty Austrian aristocrats, who pretended never to have heard of the 'foreigners' from the Rhineland.

The Count was too insensitive to notice the studied slights or to believe that his secure little world had crashed about his ears. But his wife was all too conscious of the straits to which they had come.

For herself she did not particularly mind; nor did she surmise that anything, even revolution and exile, could disturb the stupid serenity of her husband. But for her beloved son, for whom she had dreamed such dreams of greatness, the situation was tragic.

Countess Beatrice bestirred herself to do something about it. In childhood and as a young unmarried woman she had had a close girl friend, Princess von Oettingen-Spielberg. Diverging paths after their respective marriages had broken the tie. Now she contrived to revive that friendship.

All the tact, diplomacy and intrigue that Countess Beatrice had tried to teach her son was now expended with the result that the mother of the eligible Eleonore thought it delightfully romantic to envisage her daughter marrying the son of her former friend. Some discreet enquiries about Clement confirmed all the eulogies of his mother.

'The type of young man most likely to appeal to a débutante's fancy,' wrote Princess Liechtenstein, Eleonore's aunt. 'He is modest and enterprising by turns.'

Clement was in other letters to Prince Kaunitz compared to young Pitt. But before he—as an anxious father—could be suitably impressed Eleonore had made up her own mind and lost her heart.

Clement was, of course, a comparatively penniless suitor, but that hardly mattered. An heiress to the Kaunitz fortunes did not have to wed wealth. Her dowry would be more than ample for the most expensive household and the most extravagant husband.

Clement listened to his mother's plans for him coolly and objectively. Neither worried about bandying the word 'love'. It did not enter into the argument. Instead they discussed the avenues of advancement which ought to open once he became a member of the Kaunitz family.

They weighed the factors involved in the rapidly changing situation of the political scene. They calculated the financial benefits involved. They itemized the famous people who would become relatives by marriage; these were formidably impressive, and included several Royal Princes and Princesses.

Clement became deeply impressed with the possibilities. He knew that neither training nor personality would enable him to overcome the attitude of the Imperial Ministers that a Metternich was a provincial, fit only to be fobbed off with minor appointments. And even so—as the regrettable débâcle of Count Franz Georg's session in the Netherlands had proved—it were better if they were sinecures.

Marriage to Eleonore would stamp him as a Kaunitz as much as a Metternich. Privately he resented the insult to his family implicit in such an attitude and he resolved that not many years would pass before his own name would eclipse that of his wife's family.

But he was young and life was only just beginning. There was time to realize those ambitions. Until the time came he was ready enough to exploit the Kaunitz reputation to the full.

A party enabled him to observe Eleonore without more than a formal introduction and a few moments of conversation. Both the man and the girl knew, naturally, what was planned for them and each carefully but discreetly sized up the other.

Eleonore saw a tall, slim, elegant young man with blue eyes and fair hair. She thought he looked intelligent but proud and even more restrained than the etiquette of the day demanded. The very fact that of all the possible suitors to whom she had been introduced in this preliminary fashion Clement Metternich alone pretended diffidence, and even a tinge of boredom, fascinated her.

Knowing her social and financial worth she had been captious and critical about the men presented to her from the age of sixteen onwards, and her mother had at times felt both despair and anger. This time Eleonore was deeply intrigued and almost overnight she knew that she had fallen deeply in love for the first time in her life.

Clement, on the other hand, felt no emotion except the stirring of high ambition. His ideal was still personified by the lovely seductive Constance. But he was rather relieved to see that Eleonore was pretty and naturally vivacious. She was by no means sexually distasteful, though hardly up to the standards of beauty he had come to demand under the experienced tutelage of the First Gentleman of Europe and his cronies in England.

Still, one could hardly complain, he would have been prepared to put up with somebody hideous if she would, at this moment of social and financial starvation, bring him wealth and power.

Both the mothers were delighted with the reaction of their children. Eleonore's mother revealed that it was a case of love at first sight, and Countess Beatrice hastily confirmed that her son's reaction was exactly the same.

The official courtship began. Clement at first exerted all the charm of which he was capable, thereby enthralling Eleonore completely. But, with that streak of cynical cruelty which was to emerge periodically throughout his professional and private life, he occasionally relapsed into a coldness and a reserve which was indifferent almost to a point of rudeness.

If in those moments Eleonore guessed that Clement's feelings were those he expressed so frequently later in life, she said nothing.

'One marries to have children,' he would say wearily, 'not to indulge one's inclinations.'

Eleonore must often have wept bitter tears into her pillow. But she was madly in love and she believed, as every young girl before and after her has believed, that time and marriage would bring the man she loved to his knees.

As proud a girl as any in Vienna, she was by this time so completely infatuated that all she wanted to do was to give him her love.

Clement said he wanted children—and they would have to conceive them together. That was sufficient for the moment, she asked only that she could become his wife.

During these early days of courtship Clement did not reveal that he was already a father. Constance had told him, a year earlier, that she was expecting his child. She had simultaneously assured him that her husband, whatever his suspicions, would not permit his wife's honour to be besmirched by publicly branding her an adulteress and mother of a bastard.

Clement, on his side, knowing of Constance's other attachments, kept his own counsel as to whether he was or was not the father. In fact, as the child's appearance and Constance's own admission subsequently confirmed, there was no doubt at all.

When Eleonore learned from the inevitable busybody of Clement's child she was mortified and deeply upset. It would have been a natural, even desirable, proof of virility for a young aristocrat to father a few children through common women and servant girls. But this was the result of a liaison with a woman of their own class—a woman he would undoubtedly have married had she been free.

But far from drawing back from their engagement, Eleonore's only fear was that the child's paternity would become so well known that her family would, in rudimentary self-respect, forbid the marriage.

Fortunately they remained in ignorance, and the wedding was fixed for September 27th, 1795, in the little community of Austerlitz not far from Brno, a place which ten years later was to become the scene of the Empire's most terrible defeat at the hands of Napoleon.

The Kaunitz family owned vast estates in the area and they decided to hold the wedding in a modest little rural church. The Kaunitz dominance over all the affairs of the district was typified by the fact that six peasant couples had been ordered to defer or advance their wedding date so that they were married at the same time as the daughter of the Chatelaine to the young man from the far-off Rhineland.

The ceremony was followed by banquets, a pheasant shoot, by games of lotto and country dancing. Through them all Eleonore watched the bridegroom, her eyes dark and liquid with love.

It is doubtful if she remembered that through her all doors were open to Clement Metternich in the future. Riches, power, Court favour and a brilliant career were her wedding presents to him. All she asked in return was that she could, in actual fact as well as in name, become his wife.

Three

Immediately after the honeymoon the young couple set up house in Vienna. Clement profited in every way he could from his wife's social position. He was also ready to exploit his friendship with the Emperor Francis.

'Heaven,' he declared, 'has placed me near a man who seems as if he had been made from me. The Emperor Francis does not lose a word. He knows what he wishes, and his wish is always good.'

On the principle that attack on the most unassailable position was best if one was going to attack at all, the young Count, still to gain the acceptance of Viennese society, brashly launched a campaign of vilification and intrigue against Baron Thugut, the keystone of the Ministerial Establishment.

The Baron was Foreign Minister and the veteran adviser and confidante of Maria Theresa. The attack was all the more reprehensible because Thugut had been an intimate friend of Prince Kaunitz, Eleonore's illustrious grandfather and Chancellor of the Empire.

Through the Emperor and with the aid of his wife's friends Metternich set about destroying the reputation of the Grand Old Man of Austrian diplomacy. Thugut was a man of irreproachable honour. He was enormously wealthy from his business interests connected with shipping. Both facts made Metternich's innuendos about bribery and corruption absurd.

But the unfounded slanders gradually achieved their purpose. Thugut was said to be in the pay of Russia and England, while his endeavours to come to an understanding with the Revolutionaries of France was diagnosed as venal treachery instead of the realistic diplomacy it really was.

Few of Thugut's friends would have believed that a callow young man from a remote corner of the Empire could have damaged the reputation of such an established statesman. Perhaps it was this underrating of Metternich's capabilities that helped to bring him success.

It was also due to his consummate talent for what appeared to be disinterested action. Metternich was at pains to explain that so far as he was concerned politics held little attraction.

'I have no natural aptitude for intrigue,' he said. 'I detest Courts and everything to do with them . . . I don't like standing . . . I dislike fixed hours . . . I was never made for my present profession.'

He announced that he hoped to devote his life to study and research. He visited the Viennese hospitals and watched the dissection of corpses.

'I managed to surmount all squeamishness,' he said later, 'and spent much time in hospitals and the anatomy theatre. I should much have preferred not to enter public life, to spend my time in pursuit of science. Had I been a Capo d'Istria, I might have stayed where I was and become a doctor.'

In reality Clement was working vigorously to maintain his name before the Emperor as a young patriot whose services would be indispensable in the difficult years ahead. The campaign worked. When negotiations began to reach an understanding between France and the Empire, Francis II immediately invited Clement to take part.

It was, of course, impossible for an unknown young man to be given too important a role, so the Emperor appointed Count Franz Georg his personal representative and Clement as 'observer' of the interests of the Westphalian landowners.

Both appointments were made in the face of protests by the almost discredited Thugut, who had to be content with the appointment of a loyal friend of his, Count Cobenzl, in a relatively minor position to further the policy of the Imperial Foreign Ministry.

Although Count Franz Georg was, inevitably, a bumbling figurehead, he thoroughly enjoyed the ritual and ostentation of the negotiations which opened at Rastadt in December 1797.

For Clement the discussions brought little but disillusionment. Talks went on interminably between the delegates from France and the Austrian representatives. Both sides knew that the political position had reached stalemate.

Napoleon had invaded Imperial territories across the Rhine and in Italy. But the French had learned that such military activities against the primary power in Europe were very costly. While there had been several victories the campaign had not been as successful as Napoleon had hoped, and it had been expensive in men and materials.

Napoleon never troubled to go to Rastadt and his representatives had no real authority. There was, in consequence, interminable talk and no results. The French were merely playing for time to rearm and redeploy.

Clement at first visualized a contribution from himself which would produce spectacular results. When he discovered that nothing of the kind could possibly occur he lost interest and devoted himself to amusement.

'There is nothing duller under the dome of heaven than a ball at Rastadt,' he wrote to Eleonore.

This was not surprising, as there were about a hundred men, almost all Ministers, and only eight or ten women, half of them over fifty, while the local dignitaries important enough to be included in the diplomatic gatherings were not exciting.

But Clement did not write of the gambling or the suppers with actresses in private rooms with which he tried to relieve his boredom.

Many bored ladies of the Court and as many courtesans had drifted to Rastadt, drawn by the presence of wealthy and influential men, and by the glittering social life which sprang up in the fifteen months the discussions dragged on.

Clement chose a pretty actress from the Vienna Opera House as his mistress. Her name was Hanny Glaser and she had gone to Rastadt simply to find herself a wealthy protector. Clement was not wealthy compared with many of his colleagues, and in any event he had no intention of lavishing much of his money on any woman.

Hanny made the best of the situation. She took Clement as her lover but maintained herself on the gifts of an elderly gentleman who could, or so she said, be kept at a distance by hints and promises. Clement enjoyed hearing the amusing stories she told him of the way she led the old man on and then rebuffed him. But she was adamant about revealing his identity even though Clement insisted he would not be jealous.

Late one afternoon Clement was about to enter the Inn of the Brown Deer when he thought he saw Hanny in a little arbour covered with vines. Approaching nearer, he heard her laugh.

Almost silently, he drew nearer still and peeped through the foliage. He saw Hanny being kissed by an old gentleman whom he recognized instantly. It was Count Franz Georg Metternich, Emissary of His Imperial Majesty Francis II to the Congress of Rastadt—his father.

Hanny was not the only person who found the situation amusing. That winter a play was performed, entitled *The Two Klingsbergs*. It had been written by a man called Kotzebne.

As a student the dramatist had been at Mainz with Clement and they had been fierce opponents in debate in which the young Count had invariably been the victor. Now Kotzebne had his revenge, for everyone connected with the Congress recognized the satire on the two Metternichs.

Unimportant though he was in Rastadt, Clement attracted the attention of the French newspapers. An article in *Le Publiciste* said:

'Count Metternich is very young. But one can already detect his potentialities. Some day he may follow in the footsteps of his father; he might do so more quickly were he less infatuated by that personal charm which he seems to have inherited from his mother. He might also profitably realize that having been born with a silver spoon in his mouth will no longer be a substitute in the Europe of tomorrow for more solid attainments. And these are not acquired in gambling dens . . . or even in less reputable places.

'But in spite of weaknesses understandable in one so young, we find an unusually mellow personality, wit and capacities which might well some day bring him into prominence. He should not, however, mistake haughtiness for dignity, and since he himself consorts with low company he should refrain from treating certain better men disdainfully ... wherein he shows himself irresponsible, to say the least.'

The Emperor ordered the Austrian delegates back to Vienna in April 1799. Clement's affair with Hanny Glaser, which had brought him a little relief from the ennui of the Congress, ended with no regrets but many pleasant memories on both sides.

For a time no political post was available for Clement, although before he died the old Chancellor Kaunitz had recommended his grand-daughter's husband to the Emperor as 'an attractive young man, agreeable and witty, and worthy of some high diplomatic post'.

But the ultimate development for which Clement had worked so hard took place. Baron Thugut resigned, disgusted and in despair at the ruin of his policies and his own reputation.

Almost immediately the Emperor offered Clement a choice of diplomatic posts—clearly a testimonial of friendship rather than the need to find a suitable man for a particular job. Clement considered the matter carefully, knowing that this was the real start of his career. Eventually he chose the post of Plenipotentiary at the Court of the Elector of Saxony at Dresden.

While older and less imaginative men were looking West to the new regime in Paris and to the influence of London, Clement Metternich, a true European, considered that the comparatively unimportant town of Dresden offered tremendous possibilities.

It was only a few days' coach ride from Vienna. Poland, and therefore Russia, were close at hand. Berlin was nearer still.

As usual he pretended to feel humble and diffident and wrote to the Emperor:

'Your Majesty desires me to assume duties for which I feel myself little qualified; I submit, Sire, to your commands: May Your Majesty never question my goodwill—only my competence. I will do my best but Your Majesty,

I hope, will permit me to retire from the foreign service should I ever feel inadequate to my appointed task.'

It was forty-seven years before this situation came to pass and by that time Francis II had been succeeded by his son.

Metternich was twenty-eight years old when he left for Dresden. He looked even younger. Because it was necessary to arrange supervision of the estates at Austerlitz during his absence abroad Metternich encouraged his wife to remain behind, at least until he had organized their household in Dresden.

In fact, Eleonore followed him a month later, but in that time Clement was deeply involved in a new love affair, or rather in two, although he would not have regarded the second as more than physical amusement.

Clement's marriage had become, as far as he was concerned, entirely a *mariage de convenance* and he made little pretence of anything else.

In theory both husband and wife could indulge their passions as they wished, so long as there was no scandal. It was the understood thing that each should be honest and report their liaisons before some interfering gossip did so for them.

The patient and adoring Eleonore agreeed to this arrangement as all her life she was to agree with her husband whatever he suggested. Clement was probably genuine in his belief that, as he expected to be condoned for his sexual sins, so he would show the same tolerance to any infidelities on the part of his wife.

This was the usual arrangement in Vienna at that time. Many wives openly took both lover and husband to social events; some husbands even had a mistress installed in the matrimonial home.

In his own memoirs and in the accounts set down by both his friends and his enemies it always appeared that Clement Metternich was passive rather than active in the preliminaries of his affairs. His insinuation was that he was irresistible to women, who, virtuous or promiscuous, were mesmerized by the very first sight of him.

Portraits can never portray the sexual magnetism which makes this sort of thing happen among all sorts and conditions of men and women. That Clement, particularly in his young manhood, was good-looking, is true, and not even the flattering work of sycophantic artists, whose pictures often give him an almost effeminate ethereality, can wholly disguise the charm of his face.

Unfortunately we can only guess at the attractiveness of his voice and of his wit which was often barbed but could be amusing and provocative when he was gaining the friendship of a new acquaintance.

Nesselrode, then a young man but later to be the Russian Chancellor, wrote:

'Metternich certainly does not lack wit, indeed he seems to have more of that quality than almost all the other Viennese pundits put together; moreover, he is agreeable enough when he wishes, good-looking, invariably in love, but absent-minded, a characteristic even more dangerous in diplomacy than in pursuit of passion.'

One wonders if this last quality was not part of Clement's cleverness—his deliberately contrived disinterestedness?

But the real talent of Clement where love was concerned was probably his power to give women the impression that they had made the first move, and that he was an almost unwilling victim until their beauty had aroused his passions.

Once, however, he was 'captured' there was no doubt that he was a virile, experienced and satisfying lover. Perhaps the real secret of his ability to make every woman with whom he had sexual contact fall madly in love with him lay with Constance de la Force.

The wild enchantment of his initiation into the act of love had made him seek to repeat and repeat the rapture of those moments with every woman with whom he slept. He was, in fact, where women were concerned, incurably and unaffectedly romantic.

Even the most sophisticated women felt as if in his arms they learnt something they had never known before. Every woman rose with him to heights of emotional ecstasy beyond the power of expression. It was a union of the flesh which had to be shared mentally and physically by both the man and woman concerned. It was love expressed by sex which conjured up something divine and immortal. In that, as in nothing else, lay Clement Metternich's power over the women who loved him.

In the case of the major love affair Clement Metternich enjoyed at Dresden there is, however, no doubt that his mistress deliberately set out to enthral him.

Princess Katharina Bagration was twenty years old. She was the Russian-Polish wife—or rather the bride, for the marriage was very recent—of a General years older than herself. A Countess in her own right, she was, like her husband, admitted to the closest circles of the Russian Court.

Brought up in a society which followed the example of Catherine the Great, Katharina had little regard for the morals and a great regard for the place of a woman in the active political life of her country.

The Tsar—Alexander II, who had succeeded Catherine —knew all about Katharina. It was he who had encouraged her marriage to General Bagration, and it was he who had ordered his Foreign Ministry to use this effervescent and lovely girl as a spy.

Katharina was very well connected. She had Royal blood in her veins through descendancy from the family of Catherine I. She was a niece of Prince Potemkin, and on her mother's side related to many Polish aristocrats. That she avidly agreed to work as an agent of her country—and she could have had no illusions that sexual activities would be the principal requirement of that work—was a testimony to her patriotism. It was, incidentally, an excellent excuse for indulging her passions without protest from her ageing husband.

She was highly intelligent, very beautiful, and through the traces of a Mongolian ancestry blessed with a hardly definable air of Oriental mystery which made her charms unique even in the Court circles of St. Petersburg where she moved and lovely women were the rule.

A contemporary, De la Garde, wrote:

'Picture a young face white as alabaster, with cheeks of palest pink, fine features, a sweet but by no means vacuous expression, conveying sensibility. A tendency to short-sight gives her an air of timidity, something vaguely tentative, she is small but with a perfect figure, has a touch of Oriental languor added to something like Andalusian charm.'

Katharina arrived in Dresden shortly before Metternich. She had been told to make the acquaintance of the Austrian delegate who, Russian diplomats in Vienna insisted, was of far greater importance than his youth or his minor appointment suggested.

He was described on the secret files as an intimate of the Emperor and the pawn who had been responsible for the downfall of Thugut.

Strangely enough, much of this information had been given to the Russians by Kotzebne, the dramatist who had written *The Two Klingsbergs*. He had become an agent in the pay of the Imperial Russian Secret Service.

One morning soon after he had taken up his ministerial duties Clement was sitting in his study at the Legation in Dresden when he heard a carrossé come galloping up to the entrance. It drew up and someone rang the bell so fiercely that almost instinctively Clement rose to his feet and walked into the corridor.

Footmen rushed to open the door, while outside someone still clamoured imperiously for attention. Expecting one of the Imperial couriers with grave news, Clement waited apprehensively as the door was opened. There, framed in the sunlight against the dark hallway, he saw a small exquisite figure.

She was dressed in perfect taste, but her gown was so transparent that, against the sun, her body showed through the diaphanous material like a beautiful marble statue.

To Clement, standing for the moment spellbound, it

was an unexpected vision of beauty and enchantment he never forgot. Describing the first visit to his palais of Princess Katharina Bagration, he said afterwards:

'There was an Oriental softness about her, an Andalusian trace and a Parisian elegance. She was,' and his voice deepened, 'like a beautiful naked angel.'

The name stuck and Katharina lived up to it by *décolletages* which shocked even those who were careless of the proprieties.

But at the moment Katharina seemed only a child, shy and uncertain of her reception. Watching her—and in that instant desiring her—Clement forgot that he was himself not dressed to receive visitors, especially feminine ones. He was wearing only an open-necked silk shirt, and a purple velvet dressing-gown, trimmed with sable. Yet Katharina, describing him, said:

'He was Apollo descended upon earth.'

In a soft gentle voice, and with eyes which seemed a little helpless, Katharina explained that she had come to call on the countess Eleonore Metternich. With difficulty Clement forced himself to answer calmly and courteously that his wife had not yet arrived in Dresden.

The attaction between them was so powerful and so magnetic that words made little sense. They were conscious only of beating hearts and of the breath coming quickly between parted lips. They both felt as though they had been living only for this moment. They both knew the preliminaries of acquaintanceship were a waste of time.

Their affair was the wild, fiery, insatiable union of two young people crazily in love and aroused by an all-consuming passion.

Within a few weeks all Dresden knew of the attachment between the Imperial Minister from Vienna and the Princess from Imperial Russia.

Princess Czartoryska, whose salon was so important to the diplomats that she was sometimes called the Dowager Queen of Poland, declared 'they were the handsomest couple that have ever entered my house'.

And the only dissenting voice in the chorus of admiration was that of Wilhelmina of Kurland whose lovely eyes had been watching the young Minister ever since he appeared in Dresden.

Within three months of their meeting Katharina was aware that she was going to have a child. With the frankness which paved the way for him later to rely on her help, judgment and friendship in every predicament, Clement immediately informed Eleonore of what had happened.

Because she loved him to distraction, and had already trained herself to accept him as he was, there was hardly a pause before Eleonore said:

'Should it be the best solution I will take the child into our home and bring it up as our foster child.'

Clement accepted the solution without argument.

Utterly without conscience about the love children he fathered, he would have had no compunction in letting Katharina extricate herself from her problem as best she could—except for one thing. And that was that he wanted to maintain the liaison.

He knew that even for a woman of Katharina's bravado the birth of a child would present problems. She constantly mentioned that she had not set eyes on her husband for more than two years, and she left few people in doubt that even after Metternich captured her heart there were occasions when she sought affection elsewhere. Not even the tolerant circles in which she moved could go through the pretence that the baby she expected would be legitimate.

In fact, at the urgent command of the Tsar, who needed to safeguard his beautiful agent's reputation and place in society at all costs, the cuckolded husband went through the ritual of announcing that his union was shortly to be blessed with a child.

After the birth of a daughter he formally acknowledged the paternity. The Tsar was no less accommodating. Court announcements duly recorded the birth of a legitimate child in Dresden.

But Katharina had other ideas. After a brief period in which she felt rather frightened about the future, principally because she had risked the displeasure of her Royal master, she blithely told all and sundry of the expected child's paternity, while she added as an amusing example of social hypocrisy the news about her husband's reassurances and the Russian Court's congratulations on the fruitfulness of her marriage.

The idea of bearing an illegitimate child did not worry her; being a mother was not so attractive. Consequently she readily acquiesced to Clement's proposal that she should hand over the baby to his wife. The two women met to discuss details and a real friendship grew between them.

But Katharina was the type who had little sensitivity where another woman was concerned. With the official father absent in Russia, the mother was the only person consulted at the time of the baby's christening. Katharina chose and insisted on the name of Clementine for her daughter.

Clement was to love Katharina all his life. The magic of the 'naked angel' was never entirely forgotten, but at the moment the spell loosened sufficiently for him to delight in the charms of someone else, who had been determined to 'get him' since the first moment she cast eyes on him.

Wilhelmina de Biron de Kurland was one of four beautiful girls of a family identified with the Livonian Knights who brought fame and fortune to the area on the Baltic subsequently known as Latvia and now part of the Soviet Union.

Wilhelmina's family had flourished under the Polish suzerainty which had existed for more than three centuries, and it adroitly retained its position when the area came under Russian rule in 1795.

Wilhelmina had been married to a Frenchman—Prince de Rohan Guemeneé, an *émigré* who had joined the Austrian Imperial Army, his exalted birth gaining him the position of General. He was also a good soldier and absorbed in his profession—the result being that his bride was assured of the minimum of interference with her life by the presence of a husband.

In temperament and character Wilhelmina was not unlike Katharina. She too had the aura of mystery from Slav ancestors. But her appearance was very different. Wilhelmina was tall and beautiful, with golden ringlets and dark, expressive eyes. Her contrived air of cold superciliousness was helpful in disguising a desire for promiscuity which bordered on nymphomania.

She already had the making of a *femme fatale* and was to be called the 'most immoral woman of her times'. Madame de Boigne wrote of her:

'A volcano belching ice. She is past-mistress in that characteristic of northern women, combining a most disorderly life with all the outward signs of respectability.'

Wilhelmina's favours were bestowed on any man who pleased her, and there were few who did not.

Clement for the first time in his life met a woman who 'always desired what she didn't do and always did what her judgment disapproved'.

'She staggers from one folly to another, breaks the seventh commandment seven times a day and gives little more importance to love than to a good dinner.'

It was not surprising he should be intrigued, but he did not expect to be enraptured. He told a friend later that he 'accepted her as a gift'—a gift she had persistently flung at his head since she first saw him.

It seemed to Clement during the harassing days of war that when he was with Wilhelmina he stepped into another world—one of laughter, frivolity and delightful conceits.

Wilhelmina could congratulate herself that she had sampled the virility of every man of note in Dresden. She had easy means of meeting them because her mother was a leading political hostess and a source of invaluable information about every country in Central and Eastern Europe.

As far as Clement was concerned he regarded Wilhelmina as only a passing amusement between his more emotionally exciting meetings with Katharina and after the latter's pregnancy was advanced.

It is probable that neither woman minded particularly

that they had to share Clement's bed on a rota system, and there is no doubt that Wilhelmina was awaiting the boredom which she always felt for a man if a love affair with her lasted for more than a week.

But it was Wilhelmina who was to remain a constant and demanding mistress. She was often an incubus for almost the rest of Metternich's life. It was not for want of his trying to break the liaison, which at times became a source of misery, but because among the myriad of men Wilhelmina had used to distract her, only Clement could give her as a lover something she could never find with any other man.

Metternich periodically attempted to escape from her thrall. He always failed. He was made a fool of by younger and insignificant rivals but still he went back. Twenty years later he wrote:

'I gave up in much the same spirit as a mathematician might give up an attempt to square the circle. I have been as insane as that,' he said, 'trying to achieve something which by its very nature is impossible.'

Wilhelmina's hold was to develop slowly. At the outset, in Dresden, Clement's first thoughts were always for Katharina. The girl was of inestimable value to him as an interpreter of the political scene. Ably schooled by her employers, she had a piercing knowledge of facts and of the motives of the personalities involved in them.

Katharina's brief was to ascertain from this young intimate of Francis II the Empire's attitude to Poland, and the partition of that unhappy country between Russia and Prussia. Not only was the situation pregnant with the danger of hostilities but the dismemberment had brought Russia's borders deeper into Europe and made her a potential menace to Austria, always sensitive to attack from the East.

Frederick von Gentz, a journalist who later was to cause a sensation in London with his first book *The Political Conditions of Europe Before and After the French Revolution*, was afraid that under the spell of Katharina's beauty Clement would divulge State secrets.

The result was the opposite. Katharina loved Clement so much that he frequently obtained from her news of great import which he immediately transmitted to the Imperial Foreign Office.

On the other hand, Katharina's reports to the Russian Court were so flattering that the Tsar requested Vienna to make Count Metternich the next Ambassador to the Court of St. Petersburg.

Clement considered Gentz to be the cleverest propagandist of his day and secured a place for him in the Austrian Chancellery in London and a Knighthood of the Empire so that he could move in the circles where his influence would be most valuable.

Gentz, apart from the many benefits he obtained from Clement, some financial, was his sincere and faithful admirer. He wrote:

'Count Metternich was appointed under the weakest Cabinet the sun ever shone upon. Although he was hardly permitted to show a sign of life, although he was chained hand and foot, he kept his mind and his spirit, too!'

The political situation was thrusting the young Austrian diplomat into a position of influence. As usual in human affairs, the opportunity created the man—but the man also envisaged the opportunity.

As Gentz wrote:

'There is a small group of men with invincible souls who, in spite of hell and all her allies, will never lose their courage. The Austrian Minister is one of this company.'

The Electoral Court, however, had little idea that courage was necessary and they showed little anxiety about world affairs.

'To judge from this Court alone,' Metternich wrote, 'one might have believed the world was standing still.'

Russia was alarmed at the evidently irresistible force of Napoleon; so, of course, was Austria. But Russia tended to take refuge from the ominous storms moving from the West by relying on the immensity of her territories.

The defence of Central Europe would obviously be vigorously contrived by the timeless Empire founded by

Charlemagne. If its dominions should be further eroded by the troops of the Tricolor then Russia had no intention of getting involved in the holocaust—unless there were still more powerful allies.

England was, of course, an implacable enemy of France, but England was far to the West and preoccupied with sea power and the defence of the New World and the Orient. The country which really mattered was Prussia.

As regards that country, Austria's interests were identical with Russia's. Prussia was the vital link in the defensive chain protecting both the heart of the Austrian Empire and the borders of Russia.

The man to persuade Prussia to abandon her pro-French attitude and serve both Austria's and Russia's interests was, in the opinion of both powers, Count Metternich.

Late in 1803 Clement received the Imperial Command to proceed to Berlin as Austrian Minister to Frederick William III.

Frederick William, then thirty-three years old, had been King for six years. He was a reactionary and suspicious monarch, older in mind than his years, and bemused with the parlous condition of his kingdom. His father had been mentally erratic, dabbling in mysticism, and the dupe of every charlatan who cared to exert influence over him.

This corruption, Metternich quickly discovered, still flourished despite the new King's endeavours to curb it. The Foreign Ministry was so efficiently bribed by France that its officials, from its head to minor clerks, worked for France rather than the country of their birth.

Graf von Haugwitz, the Foreign Minister, was 'completely devoted to the interests of France (practically a salaried official of the State!) no longer open to bribes since the French have seen to it that nobody can outbid them'.

If the acceptance of bribes had been a form of appeasement there might have been some practical justification in it. But everyone knew that the country was in jeopardy: France was building up immense force for renewed expansion. Some believed the attack would be on England; more felt certain that Prussia or Austria would be the target.

Metternich believed in the second probability. It made his efforts to turn Prussia into an ally the more urgent. Now his really great work as a diplomat began. But, as always throughout his life, not even the most delicate and difficult negotiations prevented amorous adventures.

The attractions of Russian women tempted him to pay court to the wife of the aide-de-camp to the Tsar, Princess Dolgorouki. Her husband had been sent to Berlin at the urgent request of Katharina in a personal note to Alexander II because she believed that the two men would get on well together.

No doubt Katharina also calculated that the Princess, notoriously unfaithful, would greatly assist in strengthening the friendship. It did, and her husband was as tolerant as all the husbands Clement cuckolded.

The Princess was not the only charmer who relieved the dullness of life in Berlin. Metternich indulged in carousals as crude and tasteless as any in his life. But there was one woman who hoped for his attentions whom he spurned.

This was Madame de Staël, already nearing middle age, and living in exile in the city. As a resourceful intriguer against Napoleon, and owning a salon which attracted such intellectuals as Prussia could boast, Madame de Staël could have been of value to Metternich.

But he disliked the thrustfulness of her mind. Both Constance and Katharina had been highly intelligent women, able to discuss his problems and contribute views of value, but they were women clever enough to know that a little feminine foolishness made them all the more lovable. With them Metternich felt he was the master; with Anne Louise de Staël there was no chance of being more than the junior partner. She made him feel callow and young.

'She impresses me but does not charm me,' he observed.

Madame de Staël did not give up so easily. She pursued Clement energetically. Her wit did not amuse him and he shrank from her rough Amazonian gestures.

'I find this masculine woman overpowering,' he wrote to the Comtesse de Lieven.

Officially Metternich achieved a triumph—that it was a pointless one was no fault of his. Late in 1805 at Potsdam Prussia signed an alliance with Austria and Russia. The venal Prussian Foreign Minister assured his French masters that the treaty was a mere formality and Prussia would in time abrogate it. In fact, when the French armies marched, Prussia simply omitted to deliver the ultimatum to the French Ambassador which the treaty demanded.

Within days of the treaty being signed Napoleon had occupied Vienna, and a month later he had achieved his greatest victory at Austerlitz, on the land which, the Prince von Kaunitz being dead now, belonged to Clement and Eleonore. What was more, Bonaparte moved after the battle, an uninvited guest, into their home.

'A continuous stream poured in of the *colours* of fallen Austrian and Russian regiments,' the Prince du Talleyrand wrote. 'There were messages from Archdukes, messages from the Emperor of Austria himself and from prisoners bearing all the greatest names of the Empire.'

Seated in Clement's armchair by the fire Napoleon watched these glorious trophies being spread at his feet. That night he slept in Clement and Eleonore's marriage bed.

The already brilliant career of his unwilling host was known to Napoleon. In the days after Austerlitz, as the Little Corporal basked in the knowledge that he was master of Europe, he thought quite a lot about the man whose house and estate were his temporary home. Metternich's servants were waiting on him; Metternich's interests were reflected in the library, the pictures and the *objets d'art*.

When the time came for him to name the representative he wished to reside in Paris to preside over the interests of a technically vanquished Austria he scribbled a brief order to the Emperor in Vienna:

'Send me Count Metternich.'

Four

Clement Metternich was at a crisis in his career. The land of his birth was, to all intents and purposes, a French province and the Empire he had served had been stripped of a fifth of its domains. Berlin was unbearable, for the treachery of the Prussian Cabinet made any collaboration impossible.

He could have gone to St. Petersburg where the Tsar wanted him as Austria's envoy; he could have obtained a pleasant sinecure in the Court of Vienna. Instead he chose to accept Napoleon's invitation, or rather command, not because he was anxious, like so many politicians were, to ingratiate himself with the greatest wielder of power in the world, but because he had coolly resolved to be the implacable enemy of Napoleon and everything for which he stood.

Metternich arrived in Paris in August 1806. Despite his brooding hatred for Napoleon the usurper, he liked and admired Napoleon the man. The regard was mutual. Napoleon recognized an adversary worthy of his attention at a time when he was surrounded by lackeys deserving of nothing but contempt.

Napoleon gave the young Ambassador an audience and dazzled him with flashes of genius. This was followed by a second and Metternich realized why Napoleon was being unusually frank in his private conversations.

Austria was, for the time being, safe from complete domination because Prussia was to be conquered. But after Prussia, Metternich was convinced Austria would be the next victim in Europe.

'Napoleon fears our political principles in general,' he wrote to Vienna, 'and the Emperor's own integrity, but unfortunately has no longer any regard for our armed strength. We are certainly first on the list of victims that he feels must be immolated to his mad ambition, to his *ridiculous* system of universal domination. We are unquestionably in his way.'

After the battle of Jena Napoleon occupied Berlin, and from there, temporarily to alleviate the forebodings of Russia and Austria, he announced that his primary enemy was Britain, which was to be blockaded.

Metternich's forceful personality, and the importance of his post as Ambassador of a great power which was one of the few in the world at peace with France, rapidly turned him into a leading social figure in Paris, vying even with Napoleon for popularity and adulation.

In Paris, among the jumped-up aristocracy that Napoleon had created, Metternich, with his good breeding and social superiority, stood out. He was described as 'the thirty-four-year-old dandy, with his great blue eyes and curly blond hair'. He spoke French perfectly with scarcely an accent. He had never forgotten those first lessons on how to fascinate women that Constance de la Force had taught him on the banks of the Rhine.

What was more, he had never forgotten her. As soon as he arrived in Paris Metternich tried to get in touch with Constance, as he knew she had returned to France, but she was living far from the capital on her estates in the country.

But there were many other lovely Parisiennes ready to admire his 'remarkably handsome face', which one of his feminine admirers went on to describe as 'candid and tranquil, the eyes were as eloquent as an invariably good-tempered conversation, they inspired confidence. His demeanour was consistent with that gracious smile—half serious—and entirely in keeping with the personality of a man to whom had been confided the interests of a very great Empire.'

Apart from all this there was 'his lordly spending, the extreme elegance of his equipages and horses'. In short, Napoleon might conquer the world but Clement Metternich had conquered Paris.

The two men remained friendly. Napoleon appreciated the Ambassador's dignity, his balanced judgment and witty mind. He showered favours upon Metternich, indulged in long conversations with him and even, on one occasion, left his lunch standing for two hours.

'I am talking to you as a man for whom I have considerable regard,' Napoleon said to him in 1808. 'You have been very successful with me and are popular with people here.'

Metternich knew exactly how to answer Napoleon. Once when the Emperor had remarked that he was very young to represent the oldest monarchy in Europe, Metternich replied:

'I am exactly as old, Sire, as Your Majesty was at Austerlitz.'

But Napoleon's affability did not disguise his aggressive, warlike intentions. Metternich did not underrate his ability to destroy the remaining vestiges of the old European regime, just as Napoleon realized that the young Ambassador was a reactionary royalist who would have been delighted to destroy the Bonapartes and to restore the Bourbons.

'It would seem that nothing now can hold up the realization of the Emperor's gigantic schemes,' Metternich wrote on November 17th, 1806.

At the frank and intimate talks, at which no third person was present, Napoleon quickly realized that Metternich was incorruptible, either by offers of power and wealth or by specious arguments and veiled threats. So with his genius for ferreting out an adversary's weakness and then exploiting it Napoleon looked around for a woman to captivate the Austrian Ambassador.

He selected his sister Caroline.

Compared with the beauty and charm of Metternich's previous romantic companions Caroline Murat does not in her portraits seem to have been a very good choice. She is shown as being heavily built and proclaiming her peasant background in her thick-set body. Wealth and luxury seem to have accentuated an innate vulgarity.

But her contemporaries saw her very differently.

'When I saw her for the first time,' wrote Mademoiselle Avrillon, the first lady-in-waiting to Josephine, 'I was chiefly struck by the dazzling whiteness of her skin. She had a very handsome head, radiated good health, she was not very tall and early took on a certain *embonpoint*. Court life seemed to destroy all her charm and she looked much better *en négligée* than when dressed for formal occasions.'

As this was how Metternich saw her most often he appears, if not to fall madly in love, at least to be attracted.

'Caroline combined a charming face with unusual intelligence,' he wrote in his memoirs.

Prince Talleyrand put it more precisely when he said Caroline had 'Cromwell's head stuck on the shoulders of a pretty woman'.

In one thing everyone was agreed: Caroline Murat was very much a woman, with all the sexual fire of her Mediterranean origin, and with few qualms about indulging her passions to the limit, irrespective of convention or wisdom.

Caroline listened to her brother's pointed remarks about a liaison with the Austrian Ambassador and took special note of him at the next social event at which they were both guests.

At first sight she disliked him. Here was a man well mannered to the point of effeteness, an aesthete, and openly contemptuous of the upstarts he saw around him. Caroline's sexual tastes ran to highly masculine men. She regarded uncouthness as a sign of virility and she felt more at ease with a lover who was not obviously her superior.

'Baby-face,' she called Metternich to her brother.

Napoleon listened poker-faced, reading official papers while she prattled away.

'This Baby-face, as you call him, is important to me, and therefore to you,' he said when she had finished her complaining. 'Amuse this nincompoop—we need him at the moment.'

'A woman who traduces her husband has to be far above other women if she is to remain uncriticized,' said Caroline artfully. 'A Queen, for instance.'

Napoleon scowled. This was an all-too-familiar theme. After every conquest of a country which in fact or imagination could possibly support a puppet monarchy, Caroline had demanded the throne for her husband and herself.

States in Italy and Germany, Poland and Spain had all been cited as easily arranged kingdoms for Napoleon to distribute round his family, with Caroline and her husband having priority. She refused to see that, as soon as Napoleon had such a bauble to hand out, his brother was of necessity first choice. The present of Westphalia to Jerome Bonaparte had infuriated Caroline so that she refused to speak to the Emperor for days.

'Listening to you,' Napoleon once remarked to Caroline after one of these tantrums, 'one might think I had done you out of the inheritance of the late King, our father!'

Now, in his anxiety to have power over Metternich, Napoleon half promised that a throne would in due time be provided as a reward for the services only Caroline could render.

With this she had to be content. In fact, she saw to it that in due course the promise was redeemed.

Caroline Murat was a notable character in the tangled web of love and politics which ensnared the Napoleonic élite. Her husband had been Josephine's lover when he escorted her on a journey to Italy, delivering her into Napoleon's arms in Milan.

Bonaparte had suspected his comrade's perfidy but could obtain no proof. Determined to see that Murat should know of his displeasure Napoleon omitted his name from the list of officers to accompany him on his Egyptian campaign.

Josephine, however, persuaded the Minister of War to appoint Murat to the command of a regiment of Dragoons without consulting Napoleon at a time when Napoleon did not have supreme power over military and political appointments.

Although the love affair had been a passing amusement Napoleon never forgot the implications, and he pondered over the quandary of reconciling his attitude towards Murat, an invaluable officer but also a potential rival for Josephine's affections.

Characteristically he solved the problem of gaining control over the personal life of Murat by bringing him into his family. He told his sister, the impetuous Caroline, that he was arranging an advantageous marriage for her. Caroline was entirely amenable. Murat, informed of the plan, was suspicious and wary.

He was not a wealthy man and had no particular desire to marry anyone, not even the sister of his General. However, by dint of heavy bribes in the shape of a lavish marriage settlement and forecasts of still more promotion in the Army, he eventually agreed.

His early diffidence cleverly concealed his tremendous ambition which was unleashed once the marriage had taken place. In this he had an able partner in his wife, and the time was to come when the Murats intrigued to succeed Napoleon should he die in battle or be conveniently assassinated. But this overweening ambition was ultimately to bring Murat utter defeat and death as a traitor.

In the meantime the son of a humble innkeeper, with a flair for military strategy comparable to that of Napoleon himself, thanks to his marriage moved happily into the hierarchy of France.

Apart from the generous financial gifts, Napoleon made his new brother-in-law Governor of the Cisalpine Republic, and after his undoubtedly distinguished contributions to the victories of Jena and Austerlitz he conferred on him the title of Grand Duke of Berg and Cleves.

All this was insufficient reward for the mutual greed of husband and wife, and it was Caroline who alternately nagged and cajoled her brother until, almost in exasperation, he handed out the gift of royalty. By 1808 Murat could style himself King Joachim-Napoleon and rule over the kingdom of the Two Sicilies.

It was the politically powerful and greedy woman of this partnership whom Metternich was persuaded to make his mistress. From the onset he had no illusions that Caroline, for reasons not difficult to appreciate, was anxious for him to be her lover.

What he did not realize was that his superb gift in that direction was to make her as wildly and insatiably 'in love' with him as Wilhelmina had been.

To begin with it was just another love affair with political undertones. His mistress was under orders, while he calculated that useful information could be obtained from a woman in love.

Caroline was not as intelligent as Katharina, nor as loyal as her political masters. From her husband and her brother, as well as from other members of the Bonaparte family, she obtained information of inestimable value to Metternich, and she was willing enough to pass it on, excusing herself of disloyalty because her requests for advancement had not been fulfilled.

Metternich was amused when she asked him pointed questions about etiquette at the Viennese Court and the position of the Consort, but he treated seriously the implications that a Bonaparte was expecting to ascend the throne of some vassal kingdom in France.

He was intrigued when she told him that Napoleon's patience in awaiting Josephine's pregnancy was exhausted and that an annulment of the marriage was in the offing, and he instantly looked around to find a bride who would benefit Austria.

Under the pretext of jealousy he demanded to know who were his rivals for Caroline's favours and what the police chief Fouché and the Foreign Minister Talleyrand were doing. Caroline told him all he wanted to know. In return Caroline heard enough about Austria's policies to satisfy her brother. Metternich had quickly assessed the position and, as always, he was discreet and not above prevarication if he wished erroneous information to reach Bonaparte.

Metternich soon became bored with the vulgarities of Caroline. He was wise enough not to sever the liaison completely but he began casting around for new interest. He found it in the person of the charming and lovely Laurette Junot, Duchesse d'Abrantes.

A tiny feminine creature, as lovely as a Dresden china doll, Laurette Junot was the type of woman in whom Clement found all the romanticism, beauty and culture which he was for ever seeking in the successors to Constance de la Force.

Caroline's love for Metternich was fierce, possessive and violent. Laurette gave him tenderness and a wholly selfless adoration which was to endure throughout her whole life.

The Duc d'Abrantes was, like Murat, a comrade-in-arms of Napoleon. He had fought in the early battles and had been rewarded by Napoleon with the Governorship of Paris, and subsequently with a dukedom for success in the campaign against Portugal. And also, like Murat, he had been an intimate friend of the Empress Josephine in a desultory affair which had ended abruptly when Junot insulted her.

Josephine caught her lover in *flagrant delicto* with her maid. It may be said that Andoche Junot had a better sense of honour than his fellow officer, Murat, and he may well have adopted this brutish exploit of seduction as the only feasible way of escaping from Josephine's infatuated demands on him.

This dangerous experience of risking his head at the hands of an enraged Bonaparte did not, however, dissuade him from later pursuing Caroline Murat with energy and avidity. His efforts were amply rewarded, and the couple were regular lovers up to the moment Metternich came on the scene.

Junot's wife was perfectly aware of her husband's infidelities. The couple maintained an easy-going familiarity with one another which made for tolerance if not for understanding.

The truth was that Laurette found herself frigid with

her husband, due, no doubt, to some peculiar traits in his unstable character. He had bouts of insanity which, in time, grew steadily worse, culminating in a complete mental breakdown and eventual suicide.

Laurette was also contemptuous about her husband's intellectual and social limitations. He was a typical example of the man 'mightier with the sword than the pen', while Laurette, thirteen years her husband's junior, was highly intelligent, loquacious and very witty. She loved the social duties her husband's civil appointments involved and her salon became one of the most fashionable in Paris.

Junot, on the other hand, was awkward and uneasy in his civilian posts. He proved a poor executive and administrator and was completely out of his element in the brilliant social life Napoleon insisted was vital for the prestige of the new regime.

Metternich's affair with Laurette was motivated entirely by desire. For a time he went to great lengths to keep it secret. The Duchesse had a house at Neuilly, then an isolated and pleasant residential area a few miles down the Seine from Paris. Metternich rented a small house nearby.

Night after night he drove by cab to the river bridge. There he dismissed the driver under the pretext that he wished to stroll beside the Seine before retiring. A few hundred yards along the bank was a small gate leading into the pleasure gardens of the Junot residence. Inside was a path leading to one of those artificial grottoes popular in the 'wild' gardens of the day which contrasted with the formality of the grounds closer to the house.

On the first of many summer nights Laurette awaited him at the flower-scented grotto. What happened she recalled fully and nostalgically in her memoirs written more than twenty years later.

'Never had he said so much, yet hardly a word was spoken . . . he was on his knees before me . . . He got up to support me, his lips met mine . . . I do not know what happened but he carried me into the grotto, a few steps away, and when I came to myself again, I had committed a sin I was to expiate with tears of blood.'

Could anything appeal more to Metternich, who wanted rapture, ecstasy and perhaps tears from the woman he loved?

He took endless care to keep this love affair a secret. When he left the grotto with its soft couch covered with silk cushions at three o'clock in the morning he went to 'a house where another cab is waiting in charge of a manservant he had pretended to dismiss'.

From his two mistresses Metternich obtained information unsurpassed even by Napoleon himself on the political moves within France. In fact there was little which Napoloen did not actually keep secret about his own intentions which was not in time conveyed to their lover by Caroline and Laurette.

Many of the contents of the dossiers compiled by Fouché were reported to him by Caroline. The diplomatic moves of Prince Talleyrand were the subject of gossip in Laurette's salon, where the French Foreign Minister and Metternich struck up a close if venal friendship.

'Men like Talleyrand,' Metternich remarked on one occasion, 'are as dangerous as a two-edged sword.'

But the friendship was enhanced when Metternich arranged for his Government to present the Prince with 100,000 francs.

'Talleyrand,' wrote Metternich in January 1809, 'has taken off all masks as far as we are concerned. He now considers the Austrian cause so much his own that he seems willing to enter into all kinds of negotiations which he once refused.'

Metternich had never found it difficult to placate more than one woman at the same time. Like many men of great intellect and controlled energies he had the gift of sectionalizing his life, so that his domestic life with Eleonore, his current love affair with a specially adored mistress, and the sporadic amusement with a *demi-mondaine*, were all given the desired share of his attention but without interference one with another.

So far as he looked for personal pleasure as a relief

from his work he usually cared little for the advantages which a liaison might bring him. If he did make discreet enquiries of a fair informant it was merely because for the moment he regarded her as a source of information rather than a mistress.

The questioning was so subtle that his women rarely realized the implications. But if he felt frankness was justified then the lover temporarily retired and the diplomat discussed political affairs with a companion who was only coincidentally a woman.

But in the period of his ambassadorship in Paris this ice-cold attitude control of his mind and heart partially failed. Both Caroline and Laurette were demanding women. That each had always lived a morally lax life did not alter the fact that for Metternich they felt a love which was in the full sense of the term, *'une grande passion.'*

Wary of the dangers which an open quarrel with the rival could bring about, and considering the political and social importance of both of them, neither woman resorted to the characteristic feminine ultimatum of 'her or me'. Instead they exerted all their considerable sexual attractions to monopolize their lover to the exclusion of the rival.

Metternich, with the cynicism about women which was inevitable after his series of sophisticated affairs, believed that he could handle his love life and emerge unscathed. In fact, events showed that his judgment was for once in his life at fault. Both women, and the persons who were in their social circle, insinuated that the zenith of Napoleon's career was over.

The French people were weary of war. Metternich, writing home, said that in the theatres 'bulletins announcing victories were greeted by the applause of two or three policemen'.

The public illuminations ordered for all householders in celebration of victories in Russia appeared only on Ministries and Diplomatic buildings.

'Never was a war less national than this one,' Metternich wrote. 'The whole of France has only one opinion, one desire, one prayer, to see the collapse of her master's plans.'

The possibility of those nations of Europe still beyond the domination of French arms allying themselves in successful defence had never been so rosy. The influence of the Church was available to brand Napoleon as satanic. Metternich was convinced it needed only resolute action by Austria and Russia with their allies to topple Napoleon in the dust.

There was every justification for these views, but Metternich failed to ponder on the cogent arguments against them. He sent despatches to his Emperor in Vienna and exerted every pressure he could to create a political and military cordon against which Napoleon would hurl himself in vain and then be rejected by his own people as a failure.

For a time the outlook appeared good for the adversaries of the French. England harried and eventually decimated the French armies in the Iberian Peninsula. The Pope excommunicated Napoleon and thereby made him the implacable enemy of every devout citizen over most of Europe, French or otherwise.

The treachery of Talleyrand, who advised that Austria should wait for four or five months and then declare war, and Metternich's difficulty in getting his diplomatic mail through safely, were both contributory factors to the disaster.

The fateful day arrived. The Court, Ministers and Ambassadors were all called together in the *grande salle des Tuileries*. Everyone watched Metternich as the Emperor announced he would march on Vienna via Ratisbon and Munich.

Metternich listened with 'nobility, dignity and really admirable sangfroid'. The Emperor walked from the room and mounted a white horse in the Palace courtyard and harangued the troops. He then instructed Champagny to inform Metternich that he bore him no ill-will and that the scene he had just enacted had been designed 'for the gallery'.

'Monsieur,' Metternich replied, 'tell the Emperor, your master, that I never took him seriously.'

This pert reply, however, came home to roost.

Napoleon fought a heartbreaking campaign in Central Europe and was within an ace of defeat when he summoned all his military genius and quickly turned the tables with victory over the Austrians at Wagram.

Three months later, the Little Corporal, enjoying the palatial comfort of the Imperial Palace in Vienna, dictated his peace terms.

The Empire of Charlemagne lost more than a third of its territories. More than three million of the Emperor's subjects were handed over to France, to Russia and to the puppet German states. Rich farmlands had gone along with prosperous towns like Trieste and Salzburg. And there was a war-indemnity bill of 85,000,000 francs to be paid with the utmost promptitude.

Metternich had arrived back in Austria in time for the battle of Wagram. He found everything in chaos. The Foreign Minister, Stadion, had tendered his resignation. But, anyway, as Napoleon boasted, it was 'not a time for the diplomats and inky foxes to talk'. The matter was one for soldiers to settle.

The eclipse was utter. A lesser man would have retired, but the Emperor turned his eyes towards his young Ambassador 'fresh from the lion's den'. He saw Metternich well groomed and exquisitely dressed and found him full of confidence and optimism.

Francis gave a sigh of relief—here was one man out of his entire Court who had not lost his head. He offered Metternich the post Stadion had that moment vacated.

'I count,' he said to Metternich, 'upon the feeling you have of the gravity of the situation and upon your patriotism.'

Once more fate had taken a hand and Metternich was in the saddle.

Five

The Emperor Francis II had inherited the most glorious Empire in Christendom. Its origin in Charlemagne's triumphs had created a tradition of religious and economic domination which appeared to Charlemagne's successors —and indeed to the majority of their subjects—as divinely ordered and politically essential.

The Hapsburg dynasty from which Francis came had held the throne for so long that it was inevitable that the destiny of Austria and all her dominions should be symbolized exclusively by the crown he wore.

But faith in tradition was not enough in the restive new world of the nineteenth century. Maria Theresa, the last direct descendant of the Austrian section of the Hapsburgs, had also been the last effective ruler.

As well as being perhaps the greatest Queen continental Europe was ever to know, Maria Theresa fulfilled the traditional duty of Hapsburg women by providing plenty of offspring with whom the ruling links across Europe could be forged or renewed.

She bore sixteen children. Her son Leopold also had sixteen. Francis dutifully fathered ten, but fecundity was the only way in which he emulated his famous grandmother.

In other ways Francis failed his dynasty and failed his people. He was dull and lazy. Metternich said of him that never had a monarch to such an extent possessed 'official' entrails!

These defects of character did not prohibit him from a deep regard for kingship, but he was utterly convinced that he ruled by divine right and could continue to do so with divine help. Little personal effort was required when such advantage existed.

He instinctively adopted the role of father figure to his people and liked nothing better than to drive around his capital smilingly acknowledging the plaudits of the crowd. Francis had an uncanny natural instinct when it came to courting popularity with the masses. He never showed them anything but affability and he was an adept in the use of the current witty Viennese slang.

Without really understanding the implications Francis automatically encouraged resistance to the upstart across the Rhine simply because Hapsburgs resisted change and because Royal blood was needed to rule. In war, and on the eve of war, such idealism can be a rallying point.

But the tolerance and ignorance which Francis displayed attracted many incompetent and fawning statesmen as his advisers. No one dared advise a Hapsburg to a line of action contrary to the regal wishes. No one could risk pointing out that God is sometimes on the side of the big battalions.

Thus Francis, unfortunately encouraged by Metternich —the one man who enjoyed the intimacy of his personal friendship and had the bravery to speak his mind—drifted blissfully to the disaster of defeat.

Until the very end he could not possibly have visualized such a result. He was incapable of really comprehending the situation, clearly as it was described in military reports which all came to his desk.

They were left largely unread and rarely understood, while the King revelled in the beautiful writing of some petition or Court order concerning ritual. The seals on such documents are enormous and perfect even to this day.

They were the work of Francis, who liked to attend to seals personally, a flunkey standing patiently by with candle and mould. And the signatures are still bold and clear. Not for the Emperor was the hurried and illegible scrawl, even though the document was merely confirmation of some prison sentence on a minor offender or approval of a Court donation to a charity.

It was some blind spot in the Austrian character which made many of them become preoccupied with trivialities while the important things of life went unnoticed.

Just as Count Franz Georg had wasted his energies on the liveries and uniforms of his entourage, so the Emperor frittered away his time on seals, ranks, titles, privileges and pardons. He had lost the youth and enthusiasm which had made Metternich admire him when he first came to the throne. Now, tall, thin, his dull expressionless eyes and long angular face made him, despite his devotion to the people, a mediocre man of little consequence to his country.

Gradually he came to realize that his reign had been a failure. He was told that war had exhausted his treasury and depopulated his towns and villages. These were heavy burdens, but the real tragedy was the eclipse of the Hapsburgs on the thrones of Europe.

Wherever he looked there was a deposed monarch or consort, an heir to a non-existent throne, all Hapsburgs and relatives. It was little wonder that in the days before Metternich came to rally his hopes Francis contemplated abdication.

'I will try once more,' he said to the Burgomaster of Vienna after the battle of Wagram. 'If that is not successful I shall pack up and go.'

It was the quiet confidence of Metternich which slowly banished this despair.

'We have a great deal to restore,' Francis told him, and while he himself had nothing constructive to suggest his faith in his friend was all the impetus Metternich needed to tackle what he privately confessed to be 'incredible predicaments'.

'It is no small matter to be Foreign Secretary in Austria today,' Metternich wrote to Eleonore on November 28th, 1809. 'What happenings all around me! In the midst of what incredible predicaments have I been called upon to play the leading part: I am caught in a maelstrom.'

Yet in his own way he enjoyed it. He could never resist a challenge. He wrote to a friend:

'I shall do three times as much work, and in much less time than it has taken others—including my predecessors—to do it.'

Soon Metternich was outlining his policy for the Emperor to approve formally. Ostensibly it was one of appeasement, but he indicated that this was just a method of reserving the nation's strength for better days.

'We can only consoldiate our own position by coming to terms with victorious France. . . . Our principles remain unaltered but one cannot battle with the irrevocable. We must reserve our strength for better days and seek our immediate salvation by gentler means. . . . As from the signing of the peace, our policy will consist exclusively of tacking, avoiding commitments, and of flattery. Only so can we hope to carry on until the day of general liberation.'

The real moves during Metternich's early weeks in office were of the kind which Francis could understand and approve. The traditional methods of using Hapsburg women in matrimonial alliances were suggested. This time Metternich's idea was as bold and promising as that which had made Marie Antoinette the consort of Louis XVI. It was to put a Hapsburg at the side of the new ruler of that country.

All Europe knew of the bitter disappointment of Napoleon in Josephine's failure to bear him a child. The charge of Josephine that she, the mother of children by her previous husband, was blameless and that it was Napoleon who was sterile, had been disproved when Marie Walewska, Napoleon's new Polish mistress, had borne him a son.

But only Metternich, outside the family circle of Napoleon, knew how imminent was a divorce or annulment. Caroline had been full of it in the final days of Metternich's sojourn in Paris.

Her tongue had been loosened even more than usual because of the emotional clashes which the news aroused in her heart. Much as she disliked Josephine she dreaded even more the appearance of a new wife for her brother. There was little chance of Josephine ever having a child now that she was in her forties. Whoever replaced her would need but one dowry—the certainty of fertility.

Caroline was quite certain that Napoleon would have to try to prove this before any wedding. Thus all Caroline's dreams of her husband somehow succeeding her brother would be dashed. Not even her optimism could see any means of thwarting a direct descendant born in wedlock.

Metternich had gone to Vienna absolutely convinced that with the war over Napoleon would seek a new wife. Bonaparte's actions after the battle of Wagram confirmed his view. On the pretext that the peace negotiations needed his personal attention on the spot—though obviously the victor could insist on plenipotentiaries being sent to his own capital—he remained in the vicinity of Vienna.

With any eye to future aggrandizement and new alliances Napoleon at first favoured marriage into the family of the Tsars. Alexander had two unmarried sisters—Princess Catherine and the Grand Duchess Anne. The Romanoffs were cursed with some peculiar hereditary factors, but the girls seemed fit and healthy, and politically the advantages were tremendous.

Napoleon liked the idea the more he thought about it. Unfortunately for him, the Dowager Empress of Russia, the real power behind the Tsar's throne, loathed the very name of Napoleon. She had no intention that either of her daughters should marry a Corsican peasant and a revolutionary who had insulted or deposed every person of Royal blood in Europe.

With all her powers of claiming instant obedience from her children, she got Catherine to agree to a hurried marriage to Prince George of Oldenburg. Anne was too young for anything but a token marriage, and this her mother categorically refused to authorize. She made her son announce with the full authority of a Tsarist pronouncement that the Grand Duchess Anne was to remain single while her education continued.

Napoleon knew when he was beaten. He could not wait for Anne to grow up, nor for intrigues and threats to persuade the Tsar to alter his decision. An heir was too urgently needed.

It was at this point that Metternich got to work. Napoleon had abruptly returned to Paris. Couriers had brought Metternich secret news which indicated that a divorce was imminent.

Napoleon had ordered that the communicating door between Josephine's bedroom and his own at Fontainebleau should be bricked up. Relatives had been ordered to stand by for a family conference.

Napoleon went back to France at the end of October. It took him a month to summon the courage to tell Josephine that their marriage was over. On November 30th, 1809, they dined together in the Tuileries.

He promised her a pension of 5,000,000 francs a year and the gift of the Principality of Rome as hers to do with as she liked. He assured her that he still adored her:

'Josephine, my lovely Josephine,' he said. 'You know how much I have loved you; that to you, to you alone, I owe the little happiness I have experienced in this world. But, Josephine, my destiny is more powerful than my will; my dearest affections must yield to the interests of France...'

Josephine fell to the floor, shrieking. It was the eve of the anniversary of her Coronation as Empress of France.

Next day the divorce was formally put through in a room at the Tuileries, in the presence of Napoleon's gloating family.

At that moment Napoleon was merely ridding himself of a wife who had become an incubus. He had little idea as to whom her successor would be.

In Vienna Metternich was constantly conferring with Francis far into the night. Only the long friendship which existed between them justified the frankness of Metternich's conversation. Metternich's courage was the more real because he instinctively held his monarch in veneration, refusing to regard him as anything but Holy Roman

Emperor even though, with the defeat of the Empire, the title no longer existed and Francis was merely Emperor of Austria, and in fact a mere King.

Metternich's determination to salvage a glittering prize from the ashes of defeat drove him on to make what was, in view of the Russian monarchy's contemptuous rebuff to the upstart from France, an almost insulting suggestion.

It was that the nineteen-year-old daughter of Francis, Marie Louise, should be offered as a bride for Napoleon.

'She will avenge the Hapsburgs,' he said.

That sentence in itself was sufficient to banish almost every doubt the King had.

'The Archduchess will be ready to sacrifice herself for her people,' Francis said.

Metternich wisely omitted to stress that he hoped the girl would in fact be bartered for the return of some of Austria's lost lands, as well as to eclipse the Bonaparte heredity with the glory of Hapsburg blood.

But he had the authority he needed to start his intrigue. Immediately he got to work with all his powers of negotiations. He sent as a secretary to the Austrian Embassy in Paris a young man named Floret whom he could trust absolutely. He encouraged Eleonore, that retiring, intelligent and wonderfully loyal woman who had remained in Paris throughout the war with her children, to send him her own appreciation of the situation.

He wrote to her on January 27th, 1810:

'At the moment I consider this matter of first importance for the whole of Europe. . . . From the moment when I first heard of the dissolution of his marriage with a wife who will not easily be replaced, I began to turn over in my mind a possible successor. It was natural that first among all available princesses, Madame the Archduchess should spring to my mind. . . . I found the Emperor in this instance, as in all others, without prejudice, honourable, trustworthy, resolute, a man of principle. . . . From then on, I felt that I could safely pursue my plan.'

Eleonore met Napoleon's brother, Lucien, and she had long sympathetic talks with Josephine. She played cards with Napoleon. And in every meeting with the Bonapartes she sowed the seeds of desirability of a union with Marie Louise. Even Josephine came round to admit that if such a marriage could be arranged the sacrifice she had made would not be pure loss.

At *la Malmaison* Josephine said to Eleonore:

'I have a plan with which I am seriously preoccupied, the success of which alone would make the sacrifice I have just made appear to me worth while; I mean that the Emperor should marry your Archduchess; I spoke to him about it yesterday and he told me that his choice was not yet fixed.'

Josephine paused and smiled at Eleonore.

'I think that it could be were he sure to be accepted *chez vous*.'

'I would regard such a marriage as a great honour,' Eleonore murmured.

Napoleon was quite captivated—and not a little deceived—by Eleonore Metternich. By the time the marriage project was being seriously discussed he could comment after he had enjoyed a private talk lasting some hours:

'I like Madame de Metternich. She is a really charming woman because she never meddles in politics.'

In fact, this remarkable woman was exerting political pressure with a finesse that her husband had to applaud. And it was through Countess Metternich that Napoleon ascertained the information that the proposed marriage would receive Metternich's support.

Napoleon approached Eleonore at a masked ball given by the French Government. He was anxious to know that the insulting rebuff he had received from the Tsar would not be repeated by the King of Austria.

'If you were the Archduchess Marie Louise yourself, Madame—what would your answer be to my proposal?' he asked bluntly.

If he expected flattery he was disappointed.

'I would most assuredly refuse,' retorted Eleonore; 'until I had learned the wishes of my father and my father's Minister's.'

Napoleon gently chided her for being so cold-hearted, but he took the hint. Next day Eugene, Napoleon's stepson by marriage to Josephine, formally called on the Austrian Ambassador, Prince Schwartzenberg, and made an official proposal for the hand of Marie Louise on behalf of Napoleon.

Ahead of the dipomatic courier conveying this news to the Foreign Minister in Vienna went Eleonore's report of her conversation with Napoleon. Thus one evening Metternich was able to tell Francis that he believed all was going well. He forecast developments within a matter of hours. The arrival of the official despatch confirmed Metternich's uncanny perspicacity in the eyes of his master.

Francis wanted Metternich to make the decision. Metternich refused, telling the King that as a father and an Emperor only he could decide.

Francis, as usual, became timid when confronted with a major decision. He insisted that his daughter, though still a minor and, irrespective of age, bound by convention and law to observe discipline as regards marriage, should make up her mind for herself. Nor would he tell the girl himself; Metternich would have to do so.

Marie Louise agreed to the marriage without hesitation, once Metternich told her that her father would not disapprove.

There is no doubt that the young girl was, in fact, rather intrigued by the idea of Napoleon both as a man and as a husband. Metternich reassured Count Otto, the French Ambassador:

'We inquired as to the feelings of Madame the Archduchess in this matter some three days ago, since naturally the Emperor would never have consented to impose a distasteful union upon her, and we found our Princess *exceedingly well disposed.*'

Count Otto, in his turn, wrote later on to France:

'Madame the Archduchess has asked a number of questions which suggest the serious side of her preoccupation. ... Does the Emperor like music? ... The Emperor is so good to me, do you think he would allow me to have a botanical garden? . . . I hope the Emperor will be patient with me: I do not know how to dance quadrilles but, if he wishes, I will take a dancing master.'

Generally the Hapsburg family were delighted, steeped as they were in the conception of conquest through marriage. The only hostility came from Marie Louise's grandmother, Maria Carola, the fiery old Queen of Sicily, who hated Napoleon.

'Metternich wants to make me the devil's grandparent!' she exclaimed.

Some of the Viennese aristocracy also voiced disapproval, being 'dumbfounded' to learn that the great-granddaughter of Maria Theresa was to occupy the bed of a *soldier of fortune*, the place recently vacated by a Creole —Josephine, ex-mistress of Barras and many others.

'Nobody suspected the truth,' wrote Countess Lulu Thurheim in her memoirs. 'Nobody had considered how this new daughter of Aeneas might avenge her people— except, perhaps, one man. That man was Metternich. And Marie Louise was in fact predestined to avenge Austria.'

Lady Castlereagh put it most succinctly when she said: 'A virgin from the House of Austria had to be sacrificed to appease the monster.'

Resistance to the scheme was of course futile once Marie Louise had agreed and her father had indicated that he would not interfere. Napoleon gave the Austrians a few days to deliberate and then issued an ultimatum. A marriage contract would have to be signed within hours or the matter could be considered as dead.

Napoleon's sense of pride was at stake. To him this was not the proposal of a commoner for the hand of a Princess of ancient lineage.

When he was on Elba he said, speaking of this time:

'The Austrian Court! What treacherous tricks in connection with this marriage! Vienna, it struck me, was behaving like some middle-class mother, trying to marry her daughter to a Grand Duke.'

Consent to the marriage was signed in Paris by the Austrian Ambassador on February 6th, 1810. Napoleon was reassured about any possibility of duplicity by a personal letter from Metternich which Eleonore handed to him a few hours before the formal signing.

'At last the all-important business is accomplished,' Eleonore then wrote to her husband. 'May God be thanked and afford it His blessing! I do not want to boast but I was able to help not a little. . . . Your letter made an excellent impression on the great man who actually saw it . . . but, for heaven's sake, don't mention this. Prince Schwartzenberg knows nothing about it, and was opposed to my using it. I acted entirely out of my own little head; it was successful and that is all we need to know. But how many sleepless nights I have had! How anxious and worried I have been!'

The Austrian people were delighted with the news. They felt that it meant peace. Metternich, till then a power behind the scenes and little known to the populace, became the hero of the day as a matchmaker who coincidentally restored Austria's prestige and brought peace to Europe.

In fact, things had developed more quickly than Metternich would have wished. His flair was to make bold, risky moves and then to compromise in discussion and argument. He regarded the signatures on the contract as a preliminary to more detailed negotiations during which he would obtain great concessions for his King and country.

Napoleon followed his usual policy of demanding quick action with cancellation of all negotiations as the alternative. The result was that the best Metternich could do was to delay the official Government approval of the first agreement signed by the Ambassador, for a fortnight.

Thereafter delays were caused only by the time-lag in the transmission of messages and despatches between the two capitals. Within ten days Napoleon's emissaries were in Vienna to conduct Marie Louise on her wedding journey.

On March 13th she set out, and on March 25th she arrived at Courcelles in the Netherlands, where Napoleon met her.

Next day he rode in her carriage across the French border as far as Compiègne, where they stayed the night. They slept in the same bed, Napoleon being determined to satisfy himself of his fiancée's sexual acquiescence before the final and irrevocable step of marriage. The civil and religious ceremonies culminated in the wedding in Notre-Dame on April 2nd.

The architect of this historic marriage arrived in Paris two days later. Napoleon insisted that he should stay at the Tuileries as the personal guest of his wife and himself.

Metternich gladly accepted. His political problem overcome with the triumph of this marriage, he could now devote time to a more personal matter. In its way it was quite as formidable. During his sojourn in Austria his liaison with Caroline had been the cause of a major scandal which had set all Paris talking. Everyone expected Metternich, on his return, to act as if he had never known Caroline intimately. No one involved wished the crisis to be revived.

But Metternich's sense of humour in matters of love influenced him to take the opposite attitude. At the ostentatious balls and banquets which followed one another night after night in celebration of the marriage, Metternich chatted to his fellow guests and saw to it that an unusually plaited bracelet on his wrist could be seen below the frills of his sleeve.

The bracelet was entwined with hair. Naturally there was always someone to whisper the truth of its origin—it had been a present from Caroline.

Six

While Metternich was in Paris he had tried to keep the possessive jealousy of Caroline within bounds and still remain the lover of the beautiful and attractive Laurette d'Abrantes.

It was his old difficulty of never being able to be rid of one love affair before he started on another and the way in which the women he took to bed, even casually, fell so much in love that they were never prepared to let him go.

Caroline, now Queen of Naples, had taken to indulging in extremely unqueenly activities which would certainly not have been approved by the *beau monde* of Paris with whom she fancied herself to be a shining light. She began to spy on her lover and her rival.

On evenings when Metternich excused himself from accepting her invitations she would order a carriage, without armorial bearings, and tell the driver to drive to Neuilly and drive slowly up and down in front of Laurette's house and round by the garden entrance.

Most times she discovered nothing, either because Metternich was staying all night or because he had not visited the Duchesse.

Then one night when he left by the discreet garden gate and made his way to his rented house he was overtaken by a quickly moving carriage which stopped a little way ahead. A face appeared at the lowered window and Caroline sweetly, but with an undertone of fury in her voice, offered to drive him back to Paris.

Metternich was too much the dandy ever to appear in public except immaculate and without the slightest fault in his dress, but Caroline, who had waited three hours for this moment, peered at him in the gloom of the carriage trying to guess if he had just risen from Laurette's couch.

There was, of course, no possibility of denying where he had been, but as the night was still young Metternich insisted that the meeting had been entirely for social reasons. To convince the Queen he showed her that he was wearing on his wrist the bracelet she had given him. A man who could persuade statesmen to his point of view was reasonably adept in convincing a jealous but adoring woman—at least temporarily.

However, Caroline brooded more and more on the situation during the weeks she was deprived of Metternich's reassuring presence. She had in her service a footman called Prosper who was noted as being somewhat of a rake and very attractive to the maids in Caroline's employment.

The Queen had a talk with her butler who was an old and trusted servant and he contrived a meeting between Prosper and Laurette's lady's maid, Babette.

Prosper was supplied with plenty of money and as Babette was attractive his task was not distasteful. He soon produced results. He told Caroline that Laurette kept a bundle of letters hidden in her *secretaire*. Babette was convinced they were the love-letters of Metternich to the Duchesse.

Armed with this information Caroline saw an opportunity to destroy her rival and ensure that Metternich's affections were, in future, devoted only to herself. The opportunity came when she held a masked ball and Junot, the Duke d'Abrantes, escorting his wife, was among the guests.

During the evening a masked woman, who might have been Caroline herself, approached Junot and in a disguised voice, barely above a whisper, began commiserating with him about the infidelities of his wife. Not unnaturally, Junot angrily denied the charges.

'Go home,' whispered the woman, 'open Madame le Duchesse's *secretaire* and in the small drawer to the left you will find a packet of letters tied up with pink ribbon—then you will understand.'

Junot hastened away without telling his wife. He found the letters and spent the time reading and re-reading them until Laurette returned, mystified as to why she had been left alone at the ball.

It was not long before she knew and she gives a graphic account of what happened in her diary.

'I know all,' said Junot, grinding his teeth. 'M. de Metternich has been your lover: since he left here you have kept up an active correspondence. . . . You can commit your soul to God, you are going to die.'

Laurette said nothing, she had no defence and let her husband rage and storm. After a little while Junot changed his mind about killing her and decided to challenge Metternich to a duel.

' "Prince!" I shall say,' he shouted, ' "You have brought despair to a man who has done you no wrong, you have fouled his honour; he demands satisfaction. On February 15th I shall go to Mayence . . . any weapon will suit me, if only it will bring death to one of us." '

Still Laurette said nothing. She knew that in this mood Junot was very near to insanity. Suddenly he changed his mind again and threw himself upon her. He ripped her ball gown to shreds, biting and beating her.

'Beside himself,' Laurette writes, 'he seemed to wish to hold in his arms a blood-stained wife, half dead and torn to pieces by his hand. . . . Great heaven, what terrible embraces!'

This was not an unknown experience to Laurette, and she had suffered at Junot's hands even when he wasn't angry. The attacks always culminated in lovemaking, as they did this time. The brutality of Junot as a husband was, of course, the basic reason for her frigidity with him.

He left her room in the early hours of the morning, making protestations of love and evidently oblivious of the treachery he had discovered. As soon as he had gone Laurette locked her door.

Morning brought a saner attitude to Junot. He tried to

consider the situation with a modicum of common sense. His solution was to decide to call on Countess Metternich.

The quiet charm of Eleonore was a byword in Paris, and she was genuinely loved by everyone even at a time when she was an enemy subject moving among the very heart of the political and military organism of France. Such was her reputation for honourable behaviour that at no time had she been restricted in her movements and at no time had people deleted her name from their lists of guests.

Eleonore received Junot the moment he arrived at her house, even though it was well before mid-morning. She guessed something was wrong as soon as a servant announced his name. She had been at the masked ball the night before and had noticed that the Duke had left long before his wife.

As soon as Junot was ushered into her husband's study, where Eleonore sat at his desk, he launched out into a torrent of self-pity and curses on his unfaithful wife, and a tirade against Metternich. He even attempted to abuse Eleonore for not keeping her husband at her side and finished by cursing the meddling interference of Caroline.

As he shouted and cursed the need to destroy a faithless wife once again returned to his mind. He asked Eleonore if she did not consider that a husband with a sense of honour must take such a course.

Eleonore, concealing all embarrassment and distaste at this crisis over her husband's affairs, spoke gently and with a calmness and dignity which checked Junot's furious words and made him realize that he was being unnecessarily insulting to her.

'The role of Othello really does not suit you, M. de Duc,' she said quietly. 'It is scarcely becoming for a man whose behaviour has scandalized the whole of France to adopt such an attitude.'

'You want me to forgive her and forget?' Junot protested.

Eleonore knew of the way Junot's temper blew hot and cold with almost maniacal abruptness.

'Forget? Of course you can't,' she said. 'But forgive? Have you forgotten that you still love your beautiful wife?'

Junot was silent and Eleonore seized her advantage.

'Wait here while I get my hat and cloak,' she told him. 'Then I will come with you and talk to Laurette in your presence. After all,' she smiled, 'I'm the wife of a diplomat. I think I can help to bring opposing parties to mutual understanding.'

Junot rose and kissed her hand.

'You are an angel, Madame,' he said.

Eleonore talked to both husband and wife with forcefulness but with gentle understanding. She put an end to the quarrel and left them promising to be more considerate of each other in the future.

As she prepared to leave, Eleonore mentioned another side of the problem.

'I will try, too,' she said, 'to talk with Her Majesty the Queen of Naples and see if I can prevent this scandal from going further.'

She approached Caroline that afternoon. The Queen was hostile and uneasy. She knew that this cool and reticent Austrian was beyond her avenging arm, either through insults or political machinations. She feared the mental superiority of the wife of her lover.

She feared even more the lengths that a wronged wife, if she was a clever woman, might go to in order to thwart a rival. And Caroline was more infatuated than ever. She could not bear to think of Metternich belonging to anyone but herself.

At first Caroline took refuge in stupidity. She pretended that she did not know what Eleonore was talking about. But if she thought that Countess Metternich would find it impossible to confess that she knew her husband was unfaithful she was wrong.

'I am informed,' Eleonore said with disarming courtesy, 'that Your Majesty, for personal reasons, wishes to destroy the relationship between my husband and the Duchesse d'Abrantes.'

Caroline remained watchful and silent.

'As His Excellency's wife I should obviously be the first to take offence at the revelations of infidelity which are now known to far too many persons, though not, I am glad to say, to the country as a whole.'

Eleonore continued:

'I admit that I am a foreigner living in France and, apart from my position as the wife of a foreign diplomat, of no consequence socially. However, I am a woman, and as a woman I must tell you that I am not upset or disturbed by knowledge that my husband knows other women besides myself.'

It was a statement courageous to the point of self-inflicted pain. A woman more sensitive, more womanly, than the Queen of Naples would have both admired the speaker and taken the lesson. But not Caroline. To be spiteful she said:

'I shall not hesitate to destroy the Ambassador's reputation if he has any left. Indeed, I shall not be surprised if the newspapers get hold of the story and perhaps even copies of the letters to Madame le Duchesse.'

This was a threat and Eleonore knew that if it suited Caroline or furthered her plans she would not hesitate to give the story and the letters over to the Press, who would be delighted with such a succulent tidbit.

Metternich, as his wife knew, was on the threshold of a new phase of his career. The regard of Napoleon was vital if that phase was to be successful. Nothing could be more disastrous than a sordid scandal at this particular moment.

Early next morning Eleonore drove to Fontainebleau and begged an audience with the Emperor. Despite the fact that she was a private person—Metternich's invitation to Paris had still to be despatched—and despite the crowd of officials hoping for a few moments of Napoleon's time, Eleonore was admitted that afternoon.

Needless to say Napoleon had already been acquainted with details of the scandal. He guessed that the Countess wished to talk to him about it, but he could not estimate her motives.

Eleonore wasted no time in preamble after the usual

courtesies. She launched straight into the story, explaining what she had done and recounting exactly the conversations she had had with all three persons involved.

'It is a situation, Your Majesty,' she ended, 'which would, if it goes further, embarrass your own Imperial House just as it would injure the best interests of the Austrian Ambassador. My husband's position in Vienna is serious enough at the moment. There are many who blame him for representing too eagerly the interests of Your Majesty. Indeed it is already said in the Viennese salons that the French Emperor has two Ambassadors—his own in Vienna and another in the person of Count Metternich. A scandal involving the Queen of Naples would seriously interfere with the work on which he is engaged and well may afford considerable embarrassment to Your Majesty.'

Knowing that Eleonore's inference was absolutely correct, Napoleon felt exasperated, not for the first time, with his sister. True, he had encouraged her to entice Metternich, but he had not envisaged the enticement to be something that imprisoned the enticer.

He knew, however, that he could handle Caroline. A few strictures, a few contemptuous phrases about the peasant peeping through the regal puppet, a warning or two about future emoluments, and she would toe the line.

As for the d'Abrantes, the Duke was a nuisance except when there was a battle to fight, and his wife was much too attractive. He would pack them both off to some post as far from Paris as possible.

'You are a good little woman,' he said to Eleonore, 'and have saved me from a very difficult situation with that noisy lout Junot. You may rely on me to see that we hear no more of this matter.'

Napoleon rose and escorted Eleonore to the door. Holding her arm, he said with an almost boyish grin:

'C'est un diable—that husband of yours. It seems all the ladies of my Court have lost their heads over him.'

Eleonore smiled.

'Do you blame them?' she asked. 'I cannot see how any woman can resist him.'

That evening, back in her Paris home, Eleonore sat down and wrote to her husband:

'I do not think that your affair with Madame Junot, which has unfortunately caused a good deal of comment, need prevent your return; I actually know that no harm has been done, as regards the Emperor himself. He said, "this only goes to prove the inaccuracy of rumours which have been current about my sister".'

In another letter written seven days later on February 14th, 1810, Eleonore again referred to the incident and wrote:

'I have just returned from a visit to Princess Pauline who sent for me.... The Princess also talked to me about the fantastic Junot incident and asked me if it was really true that he tried to make a row with me. She—like everybody else—was scandalized. Goodbye, dear friend, come back to us soon.... I embrace you....'

Metternich was deeply grateful to Eleonore. It was not solely for reasons of caution that he conducted himself with reticence and discretion while he remained in Paris. He adopted the role of dutiful and attentive husband—and found it was unexpectedly pleasant.

Eleonore had always adored him and he could do no wrong in her eyes. She had always been profoundly thankful and grateful that he had married her. She had never counted the benefits she had brought him but only the joy he had given her in asking her to be his wife. Whatever anyone else might say to the contrary, she was convinced that Clement Metternich could have asked any woman in the world, however illustrious, to marry him and she would have accepted.

She understood Metternich far better than most people realized. She knew that love was as essential to him as breathing and that it must be a passionate, idealistic rapture which he would never have been able to sustain with a wife. She therefore created a role for herself which was unassailable—that of confidante and comforter.

When they were alone Metternich talked and Eleonore listened and very soon after they were married he discovered there was nothing he could not tell her. She was never shocked, never showed jealousy—although often his reminiscences must have felt like daggers in her heart.

But she had agreed never to interfere.

'When I was appointed to Dresden,' Metternich wrote, 'we decided that we would never part but agreed in certain matters to leave each other absolutely free.'

Nevertheless, because Eleonore became essential to him she had her moments of happiness.

Few people, even those closest to the Metternichs, knew how often he turned to Eleonore and became, as she wanted, a devoted husband.

On March 31st, 1798, he wrote to her:

'How I shall thank heaven when once I am with you again. I will leave you no more. I will devote all my care and all my leisure to you and my dear children.'

On April 2nd of the same year he said:

'I cannot express to you the pleasure it will give me to get back to Vienna, in the most lovely season of the year, to our little garden of which I am so fond, with you and all whom I love; you shall be very gay and we will not be separated again.'

Spasmodically all through their marriage Metternich was to write and speak to Eleonore in this way. It was usually after he had suffered from a surfeit of love and passion and, like a man who had eaten too much pâte, he longed for plain fare.

Now, once again, Eleonore was rewarded for the months of waiting, for the hours she had spent listening to the vagaries of other women, for the control she had placed on her own emotions so that she never reproached her husband or bored him.

Before Metternich returned to Vienna Eleonore was pregnant.

One strange incident revived Metternich's amorous past during these happy weeks. The Austrian Embassy gave a garden party as a finale to Napoleon's wedding celebrations. It was held on July 1st and a fanfare of trumpets announced the arrival of the bridal couple. Metternich led them through the garden where Prince Schwartzenberg had constructed a Temple of Apollo where ballet girls danced and sang in a bower of flowers and coloured lights.

There was a magnificent display of fireworks and after watching the ballet the guests moved into the concert room in the Embassy which was decorated with garlands of flowers and grapes, some real and some artificial, and illuminated with thousands of candles.

A warm wind had risen during the evening, blowing into the concert room where 1,500 nobility were assembled. It moved one of the garlands into the flame of a candle.

In an instant a blaze flared up, catching the silk-covered walls and spreading until the whole room was on fire.

The panic-stricken screams of the women mingled with the shouts of the men, all giving instructions and all seeking some avenue of escape.

Metternich was near the Emperor and Empress when the fire broke out and, with the help of Prince Schwartzenberg, conveyed them through the garden and to their carriages. Returning, Metternich saw the Queen of Westphalia was about to faint and carried her to safety. Back again, he succeeded in taking most of the French Imperial House to safety.

Eleonore and Princess Josef Schwartzenberg, the Ambassador's sister-in-law, were luckily at the other end of the concert room and so escaped easily into the garden.

Again and again Metternich returned to the now smoke-filled room, seeking victims of the first panic who had either fainted or been knocked over in the rush.

Finally, in a far corner he saw a heap of white satin. He picked the woman up in his arms and carried her into the garden. He set her down on a marble seat and as he did so the night air revived her and she raised her head. To his astonishment he found himself looking into the eyes of Constance de la Force.

She managed a faint smile and he saw she was older than in those far-off days in Strasbourg but still beautiful. It was impossible for him to stay with her—there was still work to be done. He brushed a kiss on her forehead and went back to the concert room.

Princess Pauline Schwartzenberg, the Ambassador's niece, could not be found and then while the men were searching frantically in the blazing room there were shouts from the ornamental pool in the garden.

Metternich found them dragging a blackened body from among the water-lilies. It was the corpse of Princess Pauline, and she had been drowned, presumably because she had run into the pool to put out the flames which had burnt her dress.

When dawn came several more bodies were found in the house and garden. By then Constance had long since departed and Metternich made no attempt to discover where she was living in Paris.

Those few moments when he held her in his arms and when as he bent over her he saw her smile, told him forcibly that this first great love was dead—a phase of his adolescence which now seemed centuries away.

Seven

Metternich remained in Paris for six months. It was an unconscionably long time for a Foreign Minister to be away from his post. He stayed because he believed he could there best exert his influence on Napoleon, head of the only state in Europe which at this moment mattered.

Metternich believed that he could help Marie Louise gain ascendancy over Napoleon to the infinite advantage of the country of her birth.

'The Emperor is very much in love with her,' he wrote to Francis I, 'and everything suggests to me that she is beginning to understand him perfectly. He has, perhaps, more susceptibilities than most of us, and if the Empress continues to make the best of them ... She might be able to achieve much, both for herself and for the whole of Europe. He is so much in love with her.'

Francis had been forced by Napoleon to surrender his title of Emperor of the Holy Roman Empire and was now Francis I of Austria.

In another letter he said:

'The Empress is beginning to exert a by no means negligible influence on her husband.'

This was, in fact, just wishful thinking. Marie Louise was not clever enough and Napoleon too suspicious for him ever to be influenced by a woman in affairs of State.

Metternich returned to Vienna in October 1810 with some of his glory tarnished, and he had created many enemies at home for having stayed away so long.

The concessions he had managed to obtain from Napoleon were few. The Austrians could maintain a fair-sized army and payment of war indemnities was eased. The friendly attitude Metternich had cultivated in the mind of the conqueror proved to have few ramifications of which Vienna approved.

Now that Austria was France's ally by marriage she was expected to be her ally in war. Napoleon demanded that she prepare to supply him with men and materials for his coming assault on Russia.

The extreme nationalism, born of revolution, which France typified was something Metternich hated. But France was no longer an enemy, and in the future she would be an even closer ally, for Marie Louise was pregnant.

On March 20th, 1811, the Empress gave birth to a healthy son. Francis I, the Emperor of Austria, was now the grandfather of the future ruler of France. The two countries were united by ties of blood. Once again the Hapsburg policy of 'marry and rule' had succeeded.

Such were Metternich's problems as Europe once more moved towards a war started by Napoleon. He could only ponder, intrigue and wait. And, as always, he embellished life with love.

He resumed an old liaison. Katharina had been installed by her Tsarist employers in a luxurious house in Vienna so that she could obtain information on Austria's activities and, indirectly, on France's military intentions. The seductive and highly intelligent 'naked angel' who had loved Metternich so passionately in Dresden was waiting for him now with that unique mixture of Oriental mystery and Parisienne coquetry which Metternich found irresistible.

Kathrina was able to report to St. Petersburg that Metternich was as strongly devoted to her as ever, spending most evenings and a good many nights in her company. She also wrote that her lover was strongly Francophile, his reasons being that he hoped to achieve parity of influence between France and Austria, possibly to the cost of Prussia and Russia. But, she stressed, war was not in his plans. He hoped that his influence over Napoleon would help him to thwart the latter's ambitions of aggrandizement.

But all his pacific efforts could not sway the power hunger of Napoleon. By the time winter came in 1811 it was obvious that the French were urgently preparing for the greatest military coup of all—war to the East.

Katharina's reports became more and more ominous. Austria had signed the alliance promising to supply troops for the campaign. The King had promised to confer with Napoleon in the summer at Dresden.

When, a few days after this meeting, Napoleon's Grand Armée of half a million men surged into Russia one of the defending Generals was Prince Bagration. In the weeks which followed he saw everything of which his wife had warned the Tsar come to reality with tragic inevitability. He, like so many thousands of his fellow officers and men, was killed at the battle of Borodino in September.

In Vienna Metternich read the despatches which appeared to confirm that Napoleon was conqueror of Russia. Then came the disaster of winter, so that in just one year, between October 1812, when Napoleon abandoned Moscow, to October 1813, when he was defeated at Leipzig, Metternich saw the entire situation completely change.

Now it was his task not merely to safeguard the existence of Austria as the only independent power in a continent dominated by France but to ensure that all Europe did not descend into chaos as once vanquished nations extracted their revenge and quarrelled over the looted territories of the vanquished Napoleon.

With the persistence and persuasive diplomacy of which he was a master, Metternich devoted himself to bringing a motley crowd of great rulers, petty landowners and jealous neighbours round a conference table. By September 1814 he had achieved the seemingly impossible.

The Congress of Vienna had begun.

'Pull one stone out of the structure and the whole thing will crash,' said Metternich about the ancient Empire he served. A miracle, aided by his own machinations to curb Napoleon, had kept the structure in existence. Now, at the Congress of Vienna, Metternich, in reality the ruler of Europe though never the ostensible one, set about preserving that structure for as long as possible.

He was the Great Collaborator—with enemies and friends alike, his only consideration being the Austria he served and the old-style Europe he loved.

Never before had it been considered possible that the powers of the world, great and small, could sit in conference and work out a solution to their problems. Metternich made this conception acceptable.

Not even he could have known that in the weary, exasperating months of 1814 and 1815 he was to achieve a system of collaboration and treaties which would ensure that no major war occurred, in a continent which had known nothing but war for ninety-nine years.

Two years of ceaseless work went into the creation of the Congress. It began in 1813 when he offered peace to Napoleon at a time when the Russian débâcle made France's enemies eager for revenge. At the Marcolini Palace in Dresden thirteen times Napoleon furiously challenged Metternich to do his worst. Thirteen times Metternich accepted the challenge, but only to argue again that war solved nothing; negotiation everything.

Napoleon, snarling at Metternich, regretted he had married Marie Louise.

'I had hoped to combine the present with the past. . . . I was wrong and today I realize the full extent of my mistake. It may cost me my throne, but I shall drag the whole world down with me in my fall.'

He refused to consider any reasonable terms of peace and for eight hours he and Metternich walked up and down the reception chamber.

At one moment Napoleon lost his temper and flung his hat, which he had been holding in his hand, into the corner of the room. Metternich, calm and dignified, did nothing, but waited for the Emperor to pick it up himself.

Outside in the ante-chambers the French Generals had been waiting for the Austrian Foreign Secretary to leave. Metternich passed through their ranks in silence.

Only Maréchal Berthier accompanied him to his carriage; as they parted Metternich bent forward and whispered in his ear:

'The Emperor has given me all the information that I require: he is a lost man.'

This was in the midsummer of 1813. Such a remark at that time must have seemed to be the airy hope of a chronic and impractical optimist. Napoleon had boasted that 'a man such as I am does not concern himself about the lives of millions of men'. And the millions of his armies and war plants were still proving that God was apparently on the side of the big battalions.

The people of Europe were, as a conglomeration of jealous and weakly nations, completely mesmerized by the irresistible power of Napoleon. Dire danger could stir them to temporary resistance, but event after event seemed to show that the Tricolor was invincible.

Only England had carried on the bitter struggle wholeheartedly and she had understandably been preoccupied with her own safety rather than wanting to lead a crusade against a continental usurper.

Her earlier triumphs had already sunk into the pages of history. Trafalgar had taken place eight years earlier. The great Pitt, whose example had stirred Europe to resistance, had been dead since the eve of Austerlitz. The English monarchy was degraded by the madness of the King —George III—and the frivolous extravagance of his son, the Regent.

The King's Ministers, great as their abilities were, quarrelled interminably: Pitt had bickered with Fox, and now Canning was at daggers drawn with Castlereagh. The extremes to which this sense of rivalry pushed the Government policy resulted in terrible errors of judgment and impeded military operations.

But, despite the doldrums into which Napoleon's only serious adversary seemed to have sunk after Trafalgar, Metternich was right. By 1813 the writing was on the wall: Napoleon's end was inevitable.

By the end of July England had expanded her policy of merely safeguarding the island with strong naval forces by building up huge land armies to wage war on the soil of Europe.

A rising in Spain gave the opportunity; planning provided the means to exploit it. Wellington achieved a great victory in the Pyrenees and defeated Napoleon's distinguished tactician, Soult.

A month later Wellington was storming St. Sebastian and after slow and grinding erosion of the French forces the unbelievable happened. On October 7th English troops were marching on the soil of France.

By this time England's new example had rallied Europe. In August Austria had taken up arms against France once more. The defeat of Napoleon at Leipzig soon followed.

The self-appointed master of Europe, the man ready to sacrifice millions of lives, was deposed in the spring of 1814 when the allies entered Paris. Soon he was packed off to Elba, and the misery of interminable war seemed to be over.

The time for the politicians and the diplomats to clear up the mess had come. Metternich, perhaps alone of all men of influence outside England, had envisaged how speedy would be the downfall of Napoleon.

While the Generals forced the French back and back, the man of Koblenz—raised to the dignity of an Austrian Prince two days after the news of Leipzig—proceeded with his plans for the greatest International Conference the world had ever known.

The man of peace was working to organize men and events so that his influence would be greater than that of the man of war.

With his love for the pomp and splendour of traditional rule Metternich devoted much time in Vienna to create a setting worthy of his diplomatic plans. The enormous Hofburg, the Imperial Palace, became a guest house for the rulers of Europe. Emperors and Empresses, Kings and Queens, Princes and Princesses, Archdukes and Archduchesses, lived there for months.

Opposite was the white-stone residence of Metternich built by his wife's grandfather, Kaunitz. Despite the exalted personages living across the road it was the Metternich home in the Bullhausplatz which was the nerve centre of the Congress.

Here Metternich had ordered considerable interior alterations so that the white and gold conference room had five doors through which five rulers could enter simultaneously and thus banish the difficulties of precedence.

It was the splendour of the social life which eddied round the political conferences that created the spectacle of the Congress. The Emperor Francis spent 32,000,000 florins from his private purse to augment the official budget for turning Vienna into a city of glory.

Metternich built himself a large villa in the Viennese suburb of Rennweg, near the famous Belvedere Palace. It was sufficiently distant from the Hofburg to ensure that there was no suggestion of rivalry. But in fact Rennweg emulated the Royal residence, and in importance, both social and political, it easily won.

'His great art,' Prince Talleyrand reported to Louis

XVIII, 'is going to make us lose our time, for he believes that he gains by it.'

'Strange to say, and as far as I know the first experience of its kind,' said the elderly Prince de Ligne, 'the pursuit of pleasure is here achieving peace.'

Every Monday Princess Metternich held a reception in her salon, and on that day no one of importance was to be found anywhere else. Periodically Metternich gave entertainments which exceeded in lavishness anything the Emperors and Kings could offer.

The most sensational was a fancy-dress ball at which all guests were asked to come dressed in the national costumes of the peoples of the Austrian Empire. Few of the foreigners had much idea of the verisimilitude or otherwise of these alleged replicas, and the idea was merely an excuse to appear in brilliant colours and revealing costumes.

Lady Castlereagh, by then scraggy and old, wife of the reel-dancing English delegate, looked fantastic swathed from head to foot in a gown of various colours, and wearing round her head her husband's Order of the Garter with the motto *Honi soit qui mal y pense* inscribed in diamonds on her forehead.

Beautiful women were everywhere—famous in their own right and by marriage, or notorious because of their affairs. And here Metternich, the lodestar of the Congress, was in his real element.

He was forty-one and looked at least seven years younger. Comte la Garde, representing the Prince de Ligne, has left a vivid description of Metternich at this time.

'He had finely chiselled features,' la Garde wrote, 'handsome, with a delightful smile, his face was distinguished and good-humoured. . . . He moved with elegance, had a great nobility of bearing . . . one saw at a glance that here was a man supremely gifted, by nature, with remarkable capacities of attraction.'

Another contemporary wrote:

'Nobody knows how to make better use of natural gifts.

He can entertain fifty people at once with ease and amiability without ever lapsing into the obvious ... a skilful courtier to his finger-tips; however critical or thorny a situation, he never loses mastery and poise. He has a unique flair for situations and temperaments.'

It was not surprising that for the crowds of lovely women who frittered away time at the Congress Metternich was a magnet. As he approached middle age his appeal to the other sex had not lessened. He was seeking a new love interest and he found it in Julie Zichy.

Count Karl Zichy was an undistinguished courtier who had inadvisedly joined the anti-Metternich faction after Napoleon's victory over Austria, and had thereby incurred the displeasure of his Royal master. His subsequent meek behaviour enabled him partially to restore himself to the good graces of his tolerant monarch, and therefore to find himself some sort of minor Court post during the Congress.

Wisely he missed no opportunity to praise Metternich's acumen, which possibly aroused more contempt in Metternich's mind than the previous intrigues had created dislike.

This rather ineffectual man had, however, a wife who stirred Metternich to the depths of his being. Julie was young and acknowledged as one of the loveliest women in Vienna. She was reputedly the mistress of Frederick William III of Prussia, though the rumour was based on the disbelief that any woman could reject the attentions of a King. In fact, awareness of her great beauty did not sway Julie from a profoundly moral outlook.

Something of this exaltation of spirit was mirrored in her face, and she was known as 'the Celestial Beauty'. The Viennese secret-police organization, rapidly developing in efficiency under Metternich's personal direction, checked on every rumour or tidbit of gossip irrespective of the persons involved.

A secret informer wrote on October 14th, 1813:

'Julie Zichy is too pious, too sincerely virtuous. Prince Metternich will have no success in this direction.'

Metternich found Julie was indeed as virtuous as she was reputed to be, but he did not lose interest on that account. Of all his love affairs this was perhaps the most intense and also the most innocent.

What manner of woman was it that could arouse the longings of a man in his forties, cynical in love and moving in an environment where literally hundreds of the loveliest women of Europe were ready to surrender themselves to him?

Julie was tiny. She made no attempt to increase her height either by high-heeled shoes or elaborate coiffeurs. She dressed with almost unfashionable modesty, but nothing could conceal the gracefulness of her body or the perfection of her limbs. But the magnet for every man's eyes was her face.

She had a warm little rosebud mouth, huge grey eyes set wide apart, naturally curly hair which she usually kept short enough for the curls to cluster round her head like those of a child, and a chin strong enough to correct any suggestion of weakly innocence.

It must be admitted that this childlike beauty was the symbol of something approaching a child's intellect. Julie was by no means unintelligent, but she preferred to regard life as simple and the world as she found it the best of all possible places.

Perhaps out of all the aristocratic women at the Congress, intriguing and scheming to further themselves, their husbands or their lovers, Julie was completely uninterested in the political pageant unfolding before her eyes.

When she first saw Metternich at some reception she noted his looks and his charming manners. She was quite unimpressed by the power he represented. She admired him as a person and had no qualms about revealing this opinion.

Metternich, in his turn, was utterly captivated. He had always found softness and gentleness in women appealing but all his life it had been an air of innocence which had attracted him sexually. It was Constance who had implanted in his mind that the freshness and purity of youth could give sex a rapture which was almost divine.

Katharine had that little-girl quality; so had Laurette d'Abrantes. In Julie, Metternich loved someone who was actually as pure and sinless as she looked.

The love of Julie and Metternich was something beyond the ordinary relationship of a man and a woman. She would extend her hand to be kissed when they met alone, just as she did when there were scores of people around, and she trembled at the touch of his lips.

She rode with him in the Viennese woods, sometimes dismounting so that both could walk hand in hand, like a couple of young lovers, along paths too narrow and twisting for a horse.

It was inevitable that a man of Metternich's eagerness should time and time again beg to be allowed to become her lover.

She would, without protest, allow him to kiss her hair, her cheek, her neck and sometimes her soft sweet mouth. She confessed that she adored him and was jealous of stories she heard everywhere and from everybody of his numerous mistresses.

She let him believe that one day they might belong to each other completely and absolutely, but she imposed the condition that he must give up all other women except his wife. Metternich gladly promised—and his promise was not empty. During the intensity of his love for Julie he avoided all other women.

'She loved me as only so ethereal a being can love,' he wrote later.

Ethereality was something he had never really known before. If there was to be no physical satisfaction she gave spiritual peace for his mind and his soul. After an hour or so with Julie he would return to work refreshed and in some way reinvigorated.

There is a story that Julie and Metternich went away secretly together to Weiner-Neustadt. They stayed at a hunting lodge high in the mountains, and when they arrived Metternich, tired after the work of the Congress, but still man enough to desire the woman he loved, went to Julie's bedroom.

He expected to find her asleep, but instead she was sitting up in bed reading by the light of three candles. He sat on the bed and put both her hands in his and they stared into each other's eyes.

Some strange elixir flowed from her into him. He felt his tiredness vanish, his worries disappear. Was she hypnotic or was the union of their strange and diverse hearts stronger at that moment than any physical need?

Whatever it was, at peace and refreshed yet possessed by an inexplicable elation as if he had attended High Mass, Metternich returned to his own room a little later and fell into a deep, dreamless sleep.

He was like a man who had been 'taken out of himself' by a celestial vision—a vision which had no need to be experienced by a physical union but was complete in itself.

This is the legend but it resembles too closely the real and false love of the Troubadours and the mental soulmates of the Victorian era for it to be credible. Julie was undoubtedly a good woman, but she was whole-heartedly in love with Metternich.

It is well known that sensuality and virility often go hand in hand with a desire for spirituality and mysticism. Metternich was always looking for the latter in his love affairs but this did not prevent him from being extremely sexual and being as well a magnificent lover.

If, as seems likely, he did not sleep with Julie the first night at the hunting lodge, there were other nights.

Later he wrote: 'We alone were in the secret,' and it was doubtless at that time he gave Julie a wedding ring. Her religious convictions would only have let her take Metternich as her lover if, having made him renounce all other women, she could persuade herself that they were in the eyes of God man and wife.

Their union was to Julie a marriage of two people who were meant for each other, who had been intended by Providence to meet and mate and be one for eternity.

They were, in Julie's eyes, united by 'an indissoluble

bond'. When was she disillusioned, and when did she realize that such an idyllic relationship with one woman was impossible for Metternich?

All we know is that their affair was brief in time but eternal in Metternich's memory. Soon after the Congress Julie became deeply religious and passed hours and even days in lonely self-contemplation and prayer. She died before the years could mar the glorious beauty of her face.

Among her effects was a tiny box, locked and sealed. Inside was a pile of ashes—Metternich's burned love-letters—and a ring. The ring had been broken by having been twisted until the gold snapped. At what moment had the twin souls—'mated in the sight of God'—parted and why?

While Julie turned to religious devotions Metternich characteristically returned to other women. Unconsciously he sought the greatest possible contrast to Julie and resumed his relationship with Wilhelmina, Duchesse de Sagan.

Accommodation in Vienna was difficult to obtain, and Princess Katharina Bagration occupied one half of a large residence on the Schenkengasse while the Duchesse de Sagan lived in the other.

It was ironic that the two women who were quite ruthless in giving their love to Metternich for ulterior motives should have happily shared the same house during the Congress.

Neither woman thought it necessary to suffer loneliness while Metternich was devoting all his time to adoring Julie. The Duchesse became the intimate of the leading French delegates, while Katharina dutifully carried on her espionage by becoming the mistress of Prince Charles of Bavaria—and was rewarded by the honour of entering the bed of the Tsar himself.

It was Wilhelmina who at first triumphed over her rival in regaining Metternich's attention. She was admittedly very beautiful, but she had the temper of a termagant and in her outbursts the manners of a fishwoman.

Merely to show her power over her lover she would

alternate between adoration and contempt. Sometimes she would invite him to spend the night with her and then deliberately go off with a young lover, taking care that a servant would somehow reveal the fact when Metternich arrived in her apartments.

She drove him to the limits of his patience, yet he could not, for a time, forget her. All Vienna was scandalized when he failed to arrive in time for a morning conference which had been arranged to negotiate the alliance of Bavaria and Austria.

The King of Bavaria arrived a few minutes late, as was the Royal prerogative and to ensure that non-Royal delegates were all there first—only to find that Metternich was nowhere to be found.

In a fury the King waited in his private room while emissaries dashed around Vienna to discover where the Foreign Minister could be. It was quickly revealed that he had spent the night with the Duchesse and was at that time of the morning still quarrelling with her. His voice could not be heard outside the bedroom, but the Duchesse's stream of abuse eddied down the corridor. Not unreasonably the King stalked off and the negotiations were never resumed.

Frederick von Gentz, who still worshipped at Metternich's shrine, was furious at the time he wasted in amorous brawls with 'that damnable woman'.

It was rather the same relationship that Charles II had with Barbara Castlemaine. Constantly unfaithful, greedy and avaricious, she even at times disgusted him, but she had only to look deep into his eyes for him to desire her.

Between Metternich and Wilhelmina there was a sexual link that was stronger than the iron force of his willpower. Some magnetism and a pleasure which was half pain, which only she could give him, drew him irresistibly.

Gradually, however, he came to his senses and tried to put the affair on a sensible footing. If that was impossible, he told himself, he would end it. The ultimatum he offered the Duchesse was an echo of what Julie had demanded of him—that Wilhelmina should refuse intimacy to any man but himself for six months. But to this dissolute woman the demand was as impossible as it was insulting. She rejected it; whereupon Metternich rejected her.

Metternich told friends that Wilhelmina had tried to kill herself the day after their final break. He himself was desperately unhappy for a little while, but it was not in his nature to mourn any one woman for long. There was always someone else and once again he was seeking the ecstasy which so often eluded him.

'I have never been unfaithful,' he wrote, 'the woman I love is the only woman in the world for me.'

Princess Katharina was by this time hardly in a position to welcome Metternich's return to her with unalloyed pleasure because the Tsar was being unexpectedly possessive and jealous. He had hitherto had the reputation of paying court to women and then rejecting them. This way was a method which helped him to have half a dozen lovely creatures around him simultaneously and provide him with an unwarranted reputation for virility. But at last 'the biter was bit' and he had become deeply enamoured of Katharina.

When she told Alexander that Metternich was proposing to call on her the next evening she imagined that the Tsar would be delighted to know that a valuable source of information would be forthcoming. Katharina herself was incapable of understanding why anyone should be jealous as regards sharing sexual favours. She never felt such emotions.

But Alexander was furious.

'Metternich has never loved you any more than he loved the Duchesse,' he stormed. 'He is incapable of love, that cold-blooded animal. Haven't you noticed that he has the face of a priest? That he's a man whose heart is virginal? He has never loved any woman.'

Katharina knew better, but had the good sense to keep quiet. Alexander's attitude to Metternich for the remainder of the Congress was certainly not that of a man who regarded his rival as beneath his notice.

Apart from jealousy over Katharina, the two men clashed constantly in their official lives. The Tsar, despotic head of a country where his word was absolute law, found it difficult enough to adapt himself to the regime of Vienna during the Congress.

Both in social life and at official deliberations he was treated as a monarch at least as important as the other ruling Kings and often as their senior. But there was always one rival who took precedence over him in fact if not in theory—and that rival was Metternich.

The basic hostility of Austria and Russia over the position of the countries between them meant that real agreement was impossible. And in dealing with such a master of diplomacy as Metternich the Tsar invariably lost the argument.

Enmity around the conference table was allied to open hostility in social life. Day after day and night after night there were concerts, banquets, balls and gatherings at which Metternich and the Tsar were fellow guests; very often one or other was the host.

For some time a cold, formal politeness helped partly to disguise their mutual dislike, but one day, on the eve of a ball which Metternich was giving, the two men happened to be left alone in a room.

The conversation soon became quarrelsome, ending with the Tsar drawing his sword and throwing it down on the table in front of Metternich.

'You are a rebel!' he shouted, and challenged Metternich to a duel with any weapon he cared to name. Sneeringly he added that he appreciated that a man who had never been a soldier could not be expected to be a swordsman.

It was not cowradice, of course, which made Metternich evade the challenge. Such a duel would have been utterly impossible, jeopardizing the success of the Congress and even causing war. But he was too proud to make the abject apology which would have been the only thing to give Alexander satisfaction. He used all his powers of persuasion in argument to explain that his attitude was not personal but diplomatic.

That he tried with every nerve of his body to avert diplomatic disaster was testified by Talleyrand, who said that Metternich came out of the interview 'in a state in which his intimate friends had never seen him'.

The Tsar grudgingly admitted that he was satisfied and the difficulty was smoothed over. But he was not a guest at the ball that night and never again did he address a word to Metternich at any social function at which they continued to meet day after day.

In the eyes of the Viennese, Metternich had triumphed in this dispute. Most people realized that the real reason why the two men felt personal enmity was because of their rivalry for Katharina's favours. One was the father of her child; the other her King and employer. There was little argument as to who was pre-eminent in Katharina's heart.

But to Metternich the joy of conquest, the balm of an easy, unaffected relationship free from political overtones, had gone with the advent of the Tsar as a rival in love as well as in politics.

There was no real quarrel, no definite break between Metternich and Katharina. The affair merely cooled until the very embers were dead and the 'naked angel' no longer had any power over him.

Eight

The energies Metternich expended on the Congress of Vienna exhausted him in both mind and body, if only temporarily. In retrospect he told Prince Hardenberg:

'The last few years have nearly killed me. I really need, now, to think a little of myself.'

Like any man blessed with wonderful health and an

iron constitution he worried about the smallest physical evidence of his exhaustion. He was rarely ill; his eyes troubled him and he suffered 'slight indispositions, catarrh, perhaps, or rheumatism'.

He could not but be aware that he was at the very pinnacle of his fame, and both through his record as a statesman and by the passing of the years he knew he was gaining the position of Elder Statesman.

'I have now,' he wrote in 1817, 'arrived at one of those peaks where the future may easily be deduced from the present.'

But he was always gay, always smiling, laughing, joking. In April 1819 he had his first audience with the Pope and 'made His Holiness laugh for at least a quarter of an hour'.

A year later he wrote:

'I am rather like an orange-flower, always in bloom. I am a child of the light.'

Yet in May of 1820 Lord Stewart, the English Ambassador, wrote:

'He labours without stopping, his whole mind and all his time are given to his work—he scarcely ever leaves the office.'

Deep in his heart he did not feel old, but it took him some years to throw off the feeling that youth had gone and that the adventures in love which had always been part of his life must become memories.

Whatever affairs he may have had in this period they must have been unusually discreet. Colleagues said that he was a completely changed man—and by this they meant that his amorous proclivities had been abandoned.

'Metternich is a changed man,' Lord Stewart said on another occasion. 'He is no longer what he was during the Congress in Vienna: he seems to have given up all trivial occupations; neither gambling, nor women, nor entertaining seem to interest him any more.'

Other people searched for evidence of secretive activities, and gossip produced the inevitable scandals.

It was said, for example, that he had two children by

Madame de Sagan—a boy and a girl, the former subsequently becoming Ambassador at Hamburg. But there was no evidence to prove the paternity of these children. Metternich always recognized Clementine Bagration as his daughter and she was brought up in Vienna by Eleonore and himself.

Then, in 1818, Metternich began an affair which once again seems to have had fire and passion in which he was an accomplished master. And once again the object of his devotion was part-Russian.

Countess Dorothea de Lieven was not lovely as all Metternich's other mistresses had been. But in her portrait by Lawrence he shows the elegance of her long neck, the intelligence of her eyes and the witty arch of her eyebrows. What no artist could portray was Dorothea's enthusiasm for life and her vivacity.

When she talked her black eyes sparkled and she seemed to 'light up'. Men forgot more beautiful women when they listened to her clear, gay voice.

'She impressed one by her dignity,' Talleyrand said, 'by a rather haughty graciousness, by supreme good breeding.'

Combined with this she was witty, tactful, sympathetic, perspicacious and flexible. She described herself as: 'energetic and lazy, gay and melancholy, courageous or a mere poltroon'.

It might have been the description of any well-born Russian of that time, but Dorothea de Lieven was much more. She adored politics because of the intrigue, the technique, the diplomacy and the complex struggle. As she wrote in 1823:

'I think that one wishes to live mainly out of curiosity, from a desire to know what is going to happen. I should not like to die, for instance, without knowing the results of the Congress of Vienna.'

It was helpful to Metternich at a time when he was so very conscious of his exalted position that Dorothea was socially eminent. Born into the Benckendoff family from Germany, she was related to the Romanoffs as well as being their close friend.

From birth she had lived royally, with Princes and Princesses her playmates and the Tsar and Tsarina her adult companions. At the age of fifteen she had been married to Count Lieven, the son of the governess to the Tsar Alexander, and at the time Russia's War Minister.

Significantly the Count's parental origin was considered reason enough later on to confer on him the title of Prince and Serene Highness, restricted, of course, to persons of Royal blood. It was certainly not a reward for his services, for he was completely incompetent in any post he was given.

Although the marriage was an arranged one, it was tolerably happy. Dorothea was glad of the freedom to travel which marriage permitted, and her husband was proud of her influence over the Tsar. Sent to London, she in practice became the Russian Ambassador in place of her husband who had been demoted from Minister to Ambassador.

She made an immediate impact even on the sophisticated and cynical society of Regency days. Lord Greville considered her the most blasé women he had ever met. The Prince Regent honoured her with a liaison—which she entered eagerly enough, probably because her lover was a virtual king. She was a snob and admitted it.

'I enjoy the society of Kings,' she stated once.

Metternich and Dorothea met at the Congress at Aix-la-Chapelle in October 1818. Within three weeks they were lovers and the liaison lasted for eight years almost to the day. Whatever they attempted to make it, the affair soon became more a union of intellects than of souls. Each was too impersonal, too involved in the world in which they lived, to abandon everything for love for more than a brief interlude.

Just as it was political duty which threw them together at Aix it was political advantage which maintained their affection, and the absence of those advantages which ended it.

Dorothea was not just a political servant of the Tsar as Katharina had been. She was rightly convinced of her own abilities to direct policy, and even if she did not admit the fact even to herself, her easy and immediate acquiescence to Metternich's amorous proposals was coloured by the knowledge that to have Austria's master as her lover would be of tremendous benefit to Russia.

And Metternich, in his turn, recognized and admired the brilliant mind and the unquestioned influence of Dorothea. He did not use women for his professional advantage and he did not consciously permit them to use him, but now, in middle age, he found it comfortable to love where power lay.

Dorothea was a passionate woman in her early thirties and Metternich a skilful and eager lover. An affair started unexpectedly, as Metternich's letter written on November 28th, 1918, shows:

'On October 29th,' he wrote, 'I didn't see you. On the 30th I discovered that the day before had been both cold and empty.... I forget which day it was you came to my house. But you also burned with the fever of desire, my dear, and at last you are mine! Don't ask me all that I have felt since then.'

Dorothea released on him all the throbbing passion of her Russian blood.

'Tomorrow!' she wrote to him in a promise to stay the night at his house. 'I shall love you tomorrow—as I shall love you all the remaining days of my life. My darling, how sweet it is to love you.'

Even so, their passion could not keep them from their duty. The conference at Aix ended and both of them left the town.

There were occasions in the following months when international conferences in some European town brought them together and they could be lovers, but it was rare for the period of these reunions to exceed a week.

The affair, consummated physically at appropriate and convenient intervals, was kept at boiling point by their letters. It was, in fact, their correspondence which enabled them to attain heights of passionate thought almost unsurpassed in literature.

Metternich, forty-six years of age, insisted that he had recaptured his youth.

'Such a love as ours comes only once in a lifetime,' he exulted. 'At eighteen years of age my heart was seeking what it found at forty. Am I still that cold and unapproachable fellow who so alarmed you?' he asks.

It is obvious that even the haughty Dorothea is playing up to his love of the timorous, helpless little woman who is almost afraid of his virility.

'How the man of ice melted in contact with you,' he continues.

Yet after a while Metternich began to seek a spirituality in their love, that rare elixir which almost always eluded him. He wrote that theirs was 'a sacred love—the only one worth while', and where Dorothea hoped to read praise of her love-making she found instead testimonials to the benefits of their mutual understanding and confession of his high regard for her intellect.

'What binds me more than anything to you is a kind of quiet confidence. I never question our complete understanding.'

The biggest insult to any woman hoping she had captivated a man was not omitted: Metternich told her how wonderful it would have been if she had been born a man and had had a man's opportunities for advancement.

'If you were a man you would have reached great heights. With such a head and heart as yours, nothing could have stopped you.'

Despite these indirect rebuffs Dorothea had tasted happiness in Metternich's arms. The old spell he had cast upon dozens of women captured the clever, intriguing, critical brain of Dorothea and made her like all the others. She ached, longed and yearned for Metternich as a lover. She wanted the ecstasy of surrender, the pulsating emotions of heart and body which only he could evoke.

While she was cool-hearted and intelligent enough to devote part of her letters to a commentary on the current political scene the desire for him physically always crept in somewhere.

'My darling, how sweet it is to love you. It was a wonderful experience!' she wrote in recalling a night together. Then, when she is told she will see him shortly:

'I begin to tremble all over. All the happiness, all the pain that your visit here will cause me, burst upon me at one blast. . . . My dear, to see you for so short a time, to see and lose you again, to revel but to tremble every instant of every day!'

It is clear that Dorothea was completely enraptured by Metternich. She described to him in graphic terms a dream in which they were embracing one another and she felt his heart beating against her breast. It was so loud it awoke her. 'My heart was responding to yours.'

She sent him a gold ring which was to be 'the seal of their union'. One wonders if he remembered another ring which he had given to Julie and which had symbolized their union, both spiritual and physical.

But Dorothea would let him think of no one but herself.

'Love me, my sweet Clement; love me with all your heart; day and night—and always.'

Women always wanted to tie him to them, like Caroline Murat to possess him completely, to bind him to their side.

Objects occurring in twos became to Dorothea symbols of Metternich and herself, particularly if they were permanently linked. Two trees growing side by side in the grounds of Woburn aroused her yearning sufficiently for her to describe to him her feelings as one of the trees and hoping that Metternich would have liked to imagine himself the other, growing in continual contact for centuries.

'Can you imagine us two static, two pieces of wood?' she asks.

But she was not sufficiently distraught by their separation to abandon the sort of life she had always lived. She was the intimate friend of Lord Castlereagh and used him to try to make Metternich jealous.

'If you hear anything about my supposed intimacy with Castlereagh do not conclude the worst.'

Dorothea vied with both the notorious and the famous

ladies who frequented Brighton in gaiety, but all the time she was longing for Metternich.

'Why are you not here, at Brighton, staying in the same inn or perhaps next door?' she writes almost despairingly. 'Yes, why are you not my neighbour. Everything then would be so simple.'

Loneliness, however, drove her into her husband's arms, which surprisingly enough seems to be on Metternich's advice.

'I want you to be kind, gentle, a good wife in every way to your husband,' he wrote. 'I never caused any couple to fall out. I, myself, am law-abiding and I like others to be the same.'

Ths unselfishness bore fruit, for a little later Dorothea informs Metternich that she is expecting a child, and that their meetings are for a few months out of the question.

Metternich astonishingly congratulates her warmly.

'You think I ought to be displeased to learn of your condition, or rather the cause of it?' he asks. 'My déar, what can I say? Didn't I myself urge you to be a good wife? I have no right even to wish that your husband should refrain from his normal conjugal rights. . . . You will have, I am sure, a beautiful child, you will love it and I also shall love it because it is yours.'

Before Dorothea published the correspondence between herself and Metternich this impersonal regard for his mistress was naturally not ascribed to Metternich. Most people believed the child to be his, or at least of a Royal English lover. These rumours were interrupted when the Prince Regent offered to be godfather.

But after the baby was born Metternich seemed to draw back. Perhaps Dorothea's passion was too intense; perhaps he found the 'communion of the spirit' he had advocated so strongly was not possible with someone of Dorothea's temperament.

By the time his love affair with Dorothea was a reality his position vis-à-vis Russia was beginning to change. While Austria's policy had rarely been to the advantage of Russia, except under the direst threats from Napoleon,

Metternich had personally enjoyed an excellent reputation with Tsar Alexander until the Congress of Vienna. By then the trait of insanity of the Romanoffs had begun to show, and it was this change in the Tsar's character as much as any personal action of Metternich which created a schism.

Alexander, ably tutored by modern teachers from France whose philosophies had engendered the French Revolution, had begun his reign in an enlightened manner. He instituted numerous reforms and brought some degree of liberty to his country, but by middle age his personality underwent profound changes, and the reformer became the mystical reactionary.

He methodically set about undoing much of the good he had achieved in the first fifteen years of his reign.

When Alexander was succeeded by his brother Nicholas in 1825 Metternich estimated that Russia would rapidly cease to be even an uneasy ally. The new Tsar was an uneducated boor, and his quality of unswervable honesty hardly encouraged diplomatic liaison of the kind Metternich loved.

Nicholas soon had his country engaged in war, first with Persia, then with Turkey.

As the identity of Austria's interests with Russia became obliterated so did Metternich's love for Dorothea wane. Her passionate intensity was becoming a bore. He no longer wanted to sleep with her.

In 1823, when Metternich suggested to her that she should take a holiday in Italy, enjoying the hospitality of territories which had just recently been added to Austria, she eagerly set off and made a leisurely tour of Milan, Florence, Rome and Naples, daily expecting her lover to come to her.

But there was no Metternich, and for long periods no letter from him. It was extraordinary that this proud, imperial woman could restrain her anger and write almost piteously for attention:

'So you are not coming to Italy. Then why did you ask me to come here? I left all my comforts behind, my agreeable daily round, all my interests and my friends, to live in a foreign climate which assuredly warms the body but leaves the mind blank.'

A specious excuse, a long apology or a vague promise were all that Metternich sent her—and finally no letters arrived at all.

'Where is your letter, what has become of it?' Dorothea wrote on the evening of February 12th. 'Haven't you written to me? The courier has come and gone. Ah, how wicked you are, how hateful! I wish I could send my abuse as quickly as I can say it. I am furious . . . I shall be very hostile to Austria today. . . . In short, I am going to change from an extremely good ally to the worst possible. It is very bad policy not to write to me.'

Still Metternich ignored her, and she could find no excuse for deferring her return to London any longer.

In November 1826, the eighth anniversary of the first occasion they had lain in one another's arms at Aix, the end came. She knew it was all over, but, womanlike, hoped that it could begin all over again, the past wiped out and the future rosy with the prospect of life for two who she had pleaded with him from Rome could be 'a happy and harmonious couple'.

'Let us begin once more from the beginning,' she begged. 'We should be hard put to it to find in the whole world people of our own calibre; our hearts are well matched, our minds too. . . . I repeat, you will find no one better than me. If you meet your like, show him to me.'

There was no answer. One reason was that Metternich was no longer a married man. Eleonore had died a year before and he was free. He had no desire to be tied to Dorothea.

Nine

It is significant that Metternich's star began to scintillate in the political firmament after his marriage to Eleonore, and it dimmed, never to shine again except through reflection from past glories, when she died.

There have been innumerable women who have quietly and selflessly worked and schemed to ensure their husband's greatness, but none so devotedly as Eleonore Metternich.

From early adolescence she had been offered suitors of eminence and charm. She was actually engaged when she first met Metternich. As the richest unmarried girl in the whole of the Holy Roman Empire, the bearer of an honoured name and the favourite child of the Viennese Court, she could pick and choose a husband where she wished.

Admittedly she was not very pretty. She was small and she was frail, both in fact and appearance. But she had a good brain and could use it. Her perfect manners were allied with an acute sensitivity so that she was generally regarded as an attractive companion.

Many of the conventions in which she had been reared were jettisoned when she married a young German, certainly already showing brilliant acumen and embodying charm and breeding in everything he did or said. But he was the son of a minor foreign aristocrat regarded with a mixture of humour and contempt at the Viennese Court, and he was virtually penniless.

Eleonore loved her husband with an adoration which was almost worship. She accepted anything and everything he suggested. She never complained, never protested even when she was involved in the scandal of his love life.

Men were attracted to her because she was wise, gentle

and comforting. The Marquis de Moustier, a secretary at the French Embassy in Dresden, wanted to be her lover, but he was gently refused and was content with her friendship and her affection.

More remarkable as an example of the utter devotion she felt for Metternich was the way she deliberately allowed gossip about her moral life to develop whenever he was in the throes of a more than usually blatant intrigue.

Madame de Staël was one of the few people with enough intelligence to see the motive for this. Eleonore wanted to minimize potential scandal by creating a situation where both husband and wife appeared to be going their separate ways. She thereby destroyed any animus against a promiscuous husband wronging an innocent wife.

Her love made her strive always to keep up with her husband. She kept *au fait* with every European political development whether Metternich was involved or not. She dressed beautifully and loved jewellery. She was a perfect hostess.

Despite the fact that she bore Metternich seven children her appearance and her eagerness to please did not ever greatly change from that of the young woman who had assiduously entertained guests for the purpose of introducing them to her unknown husband.

In the early days when the snobbish and suspicious Viennese Court were critically estimating the worth of the rising young diplomat Eleonore was careful to remain in the background. And when Metternich's prestige was such that nothing Eleonore could have done or said would have affected it she still kept to the role of the simple wife and mother.

'I like Madame de Metternich. She is a really charming woman because she never meddles in politics,' Napoleon had said at a time when Eleonore was personally contributing to the fate of Europe.

Napoleon had become exceedingly fond of her. He enjoyed her company and never omitted to select her as his partner at cards at some time during an evening's social gathering. In private he confided in her his thoughts and hopes—which, albeit personal, were inevitably political too.

He knew that Josephine also found Eleonore the perfect confidante. Both of them could talk to the quiet and sympathetic Austrian Countess with the certainty of getting warm understanding, good advice, and of not having mischief made of their conversations.

More than anyone else Eleonore encouraged Napoleon to proceed with his proposals of marriage with Marie Louise, and it was her reports to Metternich which enabled Austria to further the delicate negotiations to their successful conclusion. Metternich was grateful, but by then he had come to expect such help. It was usually given so diffidently and discreetly that he genuinely felt that he alone was responsible.

Her comment on the successful outcome of the Napoleon-Marie Louise wedding arrangements was one of the rare instances where she indulged in a little self-praise.

'I do not want to boast,' she had, at the time, written to her husband, 'but I was able to help a little.'

In her middle age insensitive people found Eleonore insipid and colourless. Metternich, who always had a callous streak about women once the first throes of passion were over, was harsh enough to say publicly that he could find no charm in his wife.

Perhaps her charm was fading a little. She had lived a life of strain and had lived it spiritually and emotionally alone. She knew that she was cursed with the hereditary disease of tuberculosis and she had the cruel experience of seeing the disease of her own body destroy her children.

One after another they steadily grew thin and weak. Four were dead before she herself knew that the inevitable end was not far distant from the same killer.

Metternich was devoted to his children. 'My real vocation lies in the nursery,' he said once. He was desolated when Clementine died aged thirteen. But of the four he lost from tuberculosis he mourned one with a grief that was inconsolable.

This was his elder daughter Maria Esterhazy who had been one of 'the Queens of Love and Beauty at the Congress of Vienna'.

When she died in July 1820 Metternich wrote:

'How I loved that child! And her love for me was greater than that for a father. For many years she was my best friend. I had no need to confide in her, she guessed my thoughts. She knew me better than I knew myself. . . . I constantly felt the need to bless and to thank her for belonging to me and for being what she was. I have suffered an irreparable loss.'

Eleonore must, unless she was inhuman, have felt at times desperately jealous of Maria. For here was someone at last encroaching on the place she had made for herself in Metternich's life. Here was someone who would give him what, until now, only she could give.

Yet Clement could always keep his life in separate compartments and his work went on despite, as he said himself, that 'in the throes of my great sorrow all the troubles of the world seem to be weighing me down'.

After the death of Maria he wrote:

'Yesterday, the very day my daughter died, I was obliged to attend six hours at the Council Chamber and eight at my own department. But I shall continue to do my duty; from now on, indeed, duty will supersede the joy of living for me.'

Just before Maria's death Eleonore had seen more of her husband than at any other time in their marriage.

Perhaps it was because of this that Metternich grew so vain. Eleonore's adoration was unceasing and it must be hard for a man who is worshipped as a god not to be omnipotent.

That same year he wrote to Dorothea Lieven:

'I believe that each day must add to your conviction that I am a man apart from most of my fellow men.'

He was, however, never over-modest about himself, for during the previous year he had told Dorothea:

'My soul is strong and upright, and my words are true, always and on every occasion.'

One can almost hear Eleonore confirming this, pouring out adulation at his feet every day and every moment they were together.

But the idyllic family existence was to end abruptly. Eleonore, on the advice of the doctors, had to go and live in Paris, partly because the climate of Vienna was regarded as bad for tubercular patients, and also because there were more medical experts there.

By 1824 she was too weak to go out of the house except for short rides in the carriage.

Metternich remained in Vienna. He did not go to Paris to Eleonore despite the more and more alarming tone of the letters which came from his son and his friends.

'My wife's illness grieves me more than anything else on earth,' he told them. But there was always the question of diplomacy.

'Were I to go to Paris, it might produce a bad effect on Canning,' he wrote; 'he would certainly find some pretext for my journey apart from its real and sad—and only—motive. But what he thinks is really a matter of indifference to me, and of course it might not even have any repercussions.'

Eleonore grew worse and Metternich eventually reached Paris in 1825 in time to be at her bedside just before she died.

'The French Press is busy with my arrival here,' he wrote, 'they are making their own comments. At London, even more importance is attached to my sudden appearance in the rival capital.'

If Eleonore had known of his diplomatic misgivings she would have understood. She had lived with such situations all her life. For her personally it was sufficient that Metternich was with her at the end.

She saw, not merely her husband, but the uncrowned King of Europe and the saviour of Austria. Perhaps this was her reward. Her love of Metternich had always been indivisible from the love of her country.

Metternich wrote of 'that beautiful soul who has gone

to heaven, returning to the bosom of God with a gentle and quiet confidence in His fatherly goodness'.

Eleonore would have been moved to tears at these words and she would also, after thirty years, have understood why Metternich should have concluded his letter with:

'My presence here cannot fail to have good results.'

Although Eleonore had always been in the background of his life Metternich found she left a bigger gap than he had believed possible. For the first time she was not there to listen to him. He could not visualize life without her waiting for his arrival, watching for him with adoring eyes.

He could hardly believe it, but he was lonely. Instinctively he began to search for a new love.

Ten

Metternich was fifty-two when his wife died. There were many years of life ahead of him, but he was beginning to look old.

His hair was going white and signs of deafness had begun. He could no longer subject his eyes to hours of strain as he read interminable reports. But these physical indications of deterioration were of minor importance compared with the trends of the world in which he lived.

The seeds scattered in France in 1789 were flourishing despite the wars and the defeat of Napoleon. The liberal outlook was rising everywhere, heralding unrest.

Metternich's triumph at the Congress of Vienna had been to restore the *status quo*. Whether he honestly believed that the Holy Alliance he had instituted in 1815 was of divine inspiration is a matter for conjecture.

What was quickly made obvious was that its purpose of conserving religion, peace and justice in Europe was merely the ostensible one. In practice it meant the repression of any development towards constitutional government.

Metternich doubtless honestly believed that the ordinary people were unfit to choose their leaders, let alone to lead themselves. As regards many of the countries which joined his alliance this view was right, although neither the Pope nor the King of England would join it.

Metternich was too wise and too astute a statesman not to realize that in the ten years since the Congress of Vienna his grandiose triumph had become tarnished. He saw the signs of coming fragmentation and they intensified his personal loneliness.

This was a condition of mind and not of environment. His days were busy with official duties and he could still work long hours, tackling a major problem while deliberating on a host of minor ones at the same time. Social life was as brilliant as ever, and as a widower he was asked out even more often than before.

It was at one of the endless receptions which went on until the early hours of the morning that he was first attracted to a beautiful girl—a young Viennese with a touch of Italian blood. It was a proof of that advance of liberalism which Metternich so despised that the girl was a guest at an entertainment patronized by the Austrian Chancellor.

Marie Antoinette von Leykham was only a Baroness in a society where etiquette expected an acceptable woman to be a Princess, Duchess or Countess.

But she had that unassailable asset for any woman— superb beauty. At twenty-one she was at the very peak of her beauty—'lovely as an angel and angelic in every way'.

Her figure was perfect, full yet proportionate to her petite frame. Her face was oval, with wide-set eyes, a retroussé nose, a small rosebud mouth and blonde curls. At a time when cosmetics were being quite lavishly used her colouring was absolutely natural.

As a matter of routine politeness she was introduced to Metternich. She curtsied to him demurely and he brushed the back of her hand with his lips. There was no further social contact.

A few evenings later they met again. This time Metternich kept her in conversation after the usual exchange of courtesies. To his delight he discovered that, while Marie Antoinette was duly impressed by the interest of the highest Minister in the Empire, she was neither tongue-tied nor full of idle, obsequious chatter.

She confessed that she had no knowledge of politics and little interest in them, but in the world of the arts she could talk with knowledge and an innate good taste. Better, when Metternich mentioned some episode from the world of politics, she showed that she had a lively and intelligent mind able to grasp the implications of what he said and eager for further information.

Metternich's courtship began there and then. At first he pleaded for the balm and stimulation that the companionship of youth could give him.

'I'm not blind to the facts of my years,' he wrote in his diary where he set down his most intimate feelings, 'and I am no longer actuated by the fatal ascendancy of passion —my heart is warm and calm, serene and austere. . . . I have a terrible hunger for repose—that is my heart's real secret.'

It wasn't.

The real secret was that his heart had been stimulated with all the fire of youthful adoration. He yearned for Marie Antoinette's mere presence. He craved for the briefest glance from her sparkling eyes. He wanted beyond everything to know she was beside him.

Work was sometimes neglected so that he could find time to ride with her in the Viennese woods, take her along the banks of the Danube or sit for hours with her over luncheon. He was desperately in love and though Marie Antoinette gave him no cause for a moment of jealousy, he was like a callow youth in his sense of insecurity and the fear of having hopes that would be dashed.

His friends and colleagues were alarmed at the signs. Largely the criticism arose from the fact that every middle-aged widow, every mother of an unattached daughter from twenty to thirty, realized that the Widower Metternich was a matrimonial catch of the first order.

But for others the possibility of a marriage between Matternich and his young Baroness gave rise to genuine distaste for a socially unacceptable union.

Princess Lieven, still smarting over the way she had been dropped, caustically commented: 'The Chevalier of the Holy Alliance is about to make a mésalliance.'

It was true only so far as the stilted rules about rank of the Viennese Court made the union rather unconventional. By the narrow standards of the Court, where everyone could—or pretended to—trace their ancestry back on an exalted plane into the dim years of the Middle Ages, Marie Antoinette was an upstart.

In fact her parental ancestors had for generations been devoted servants of European princelings, regularly entrusted with important office. Her grandfather had been the confidante and principal assistant of old Kaunitz himself and had known Metternich's mother when she was a tiny child. He had died full of honours in service to his country, praised by his employer.

It was perhaps regrettable that Marie Antoinette's parents had made a love match. Her father had wooed and won an Italian singer, famous as a prima donna and even more as a southern Italian beauty. In middle age she had perhaps been a little indiscreet in welcoming to her home all sorts and conditions of men and women, her criterion being not their rank or birth but their love of music.

But for an Italian woman living in a country always basically hostile to the people beyond the Brenner it was a case of either suffering a sort of general ostracism or revelling in the music she loved.

It was all the more galling to some of the ladies of Viennese society that Baroness von Leykham, whose husband held a diplomatic post which involved hard work rather than being the usual sinecure, was exceedingly popular with members of the foreign missions in the city.

The Ambassadors and the first secretaries from countries where the new spirit of the common man was flourishing appeared to enjoy the musical evenings in the von Leykham household. They were indeed far more amusing than the stilted entertainments of the Court officials, where one was always in danger of being snubbed for daring to address someone whose rank was such that they could not reply to a commoner.

Metternich was perfectly aware of the gossip which was going on. A few friends used their intimacy as a reason for warning him that an affair was one thing, marriage another. They hinted that if he formally announced his engagement the world would laugh at this proof of senile infatuation.

It was a cunning attack. Metternich, like so many men who have exulted in their virility and potency, was bemused with forebodings of old age and all that it was supposed to cause.

He lived in an era when it was universally believed that the human male underwent a decline in sexual activity precisely as women did, though perhaps a little later. As the majority of women were then in the menopause in their forties, the delay admitted for the male was not of much comfort to a man in his fifties.

But his love for Marie Antoinette was great enough to restore his old fire.

'You know me and you know how I work,' he said to his critics. 'When it comes to important decisions I consult no one. I put myself right with my conscience and that's enough.'

The fate of Kings and nations had depended on that untrammelled judgment for nearly thirty years. Even occasional disaster had not altered his view that he had been right. He applied the same attitude to his personal future.

In the midst of the hostile criticism he had one unquestioning friend: his Emperor. Francis was delighted that his old friend and devoted servant was going to marry again.

'My wedding gift to you will be something for you to see on the great day,' he told Metternich. 'Meantime I can give you an engagement present. A woman capable of interesting my chief Minister is clearly a remarkable person. As such, my Court needs her presence in an appropriate rank. She shall be a Countess. Choose the title and the document shall be drawn up.'

Metternich chose the name of Beilstein, after one of the most ancient estates of his family, in Bohemia. It had been given for services rendered by the Metter Knights in the Middle Ages, and it thereby endowed his fiancée with all the prestige of ancient lineage and tradition.

The Emperor wanted the marriage to be a public ceremony attended by the Court, but Metternich surprisingly rejected this. He wanted a quiet wedding attended only by members of their families.

On a dull, cold day in November 1827 the simple marriage took place at Hetzendorff, a tiny hamlet in danger of being swallowed up by Vienna. It had sentimental touches for both bride and groom; they had often walked there during the summer of 1825 when Metternich had first declared his love.

It was of great satisfaction to Metternich that his mother was able to attend. She was very old but still fiercely ambitious for her son. In her estimation Clement could still attain greater heights.

Metternich was grateful that by coming to the wedding she signified her approval of his marriage. Her sister, the Duchess of Württemberg, was also present and the doors of the church were locked during the ceremony to prevent social climbers and local villagers from attending.

Once the wedding was over and the marriage an accomplished fact Metternich dispensed with all secretiveness. He had always loved social life and considered dinners and balls an essential side of his profession. Now he launched into entertainment for its own sake—and to introduce his lovely young wife to society.

With the doting anxiety to please of an utterly enraptured lover he agreed to every idea of Marie Antoinette's to modernize the Chancellor's Palace. She was extravagant and spent vast sums of money completely refurnishing some of the rooms.

Metternich changed from his old practice of putting work before everything else and sat by her side as she interviewed cabinet-makers, designers and textile merchants. When a decision was difficult between two items he always insisted that the criterion should be which was the most expensive—and that must be the choice.

Many of his new mother-in-law's friends from the opera and concert hall came both as guests and performers. Marie Antoinette's musical taste was good, but no musical evening was arranged solely because of its cultural value. She demanded gaiety and freshness.

There was laughter in the Metternich Palace, and there was great happiness. A few of the old guard were disgusted and not even the enthusiasm of the Royal Family for an evening at the Metternichs' home could persuade them to approve. But for the overwhelming majority of people, both Viennese and among the diplomatic representatives, the Chancellor and his scintillating young wife became the most popular hosts in the city.

The politican who had devoted a lifetime to disguising his real feelings now acted like an ingenuous youth. He would put his arm round his wife's waist as they sat talking with guests. He would fuss over her, follow her with his eyes when she moved away and apologize a little later for not having heard what a guest had been saying.

But his watching eyes never found another to arouse his jealousy. He knew, and the wonder of it never ceased to make him marvel, that Marie Antoinette was as deeply in love with him as he was with her.

'I have found what I have spent a lifetime looking for,' he told Francis. 'A human being who would belong to me entirely and for whom I need never suffer a pang of regret nor a moment of jealousy.'

The happy, hectic round of social activity continued right through the winter and through the summer. It continued long after the carping critics had found a new reason to complain that not merely good behaviour, but basic decency, was being flaunted.

Marie Antoinette was obviously pregnant and still entertaining. She did not try to conceal the fact, and in any event her delighted husband informed all and sundry. He not only smilingly praised his own virility but made joking rebukes to his men friends who, he claimed, had probably made wagers that paternity was something not even a Metternich could accomplish.

During the final weeks of her waiting time Marie Antoinette enjoyed the unremitting attention and companionship of her husband. She felt wonderfully well and happy and he teased her about her size.

'I'm sure I shall bear twins,' she smiled.

'Not twins,' said Metternich, 'but a fine, big boy—our son—my son.'

The baby was indeed a boy—a fat, vigorous child. But the dazzling, exuberant Marie Antoinette died giving him birth.

Metternich was prostrated with grief, but strangely humbled and fatalistic as if he had known all along that the ecstatic happiness which he had found in his young wife could not possibly last.

He sat at his desk for hours after he had kissed her closed eyes. State documents which had accumulated for two days were ignored. He pulled his diary towards him and began to set down his thoughts.

'A most horrible calamity has fallen upon me. What God gave, He has the right to take away—man can only bow his head and not question. I believe ... and I worship His immutable decrees.'

In the yearning for someone in whom to confide he turned, as he periodically did, to writing to Princess Lieven—a correspondent who had been ignored after her gibe about his mésalliance. Now that he was alone once more he needed to sense the sympathy which his one-time mistress could, if she chose, give him.

'I have suffered the most terrible blow that fate could possibly deal me,' he wrote. 'I have lost more than half my life. I have lost my home, my domestic happiness, all that part of my life which really belonged to me, the part which helped me to bear the rest—which is not mine; everything for me has crumbled.'

He tried to rally his courage but it was almost impossible.

'My life is finished,' he wrote in another letter, 'and if I am not physically reckoned among the dead, in the spirit I am now enrolled in that great army.'

He still had his baby son, whom he named Richard. The child was 'fat and very ugly, healthy and well set-up'.

Perhaps it was the nursery where he had always been completely at home that Metternich's amazing vitality was triumphantly resurrected. He found his life was by no means finished.

Eleven

There was one woman who could not suppress a feeling of exultation at the news of Marie Antoinette's death. Her name was Countess Molly von Zichy-Ferraris, 'a very cultured great lady, true friend, loyal and discreet, a heart of gold, high-principled, sensitive and generous'.

The wife of an immensely wealthy Hungarian landowner and merchant, with some Turkish blood in his veins, Countess Molly was the arbiter of social life in the capital and thus throughout the country.

She imposed her unwritten laws with a ruthlessness which made it utterly impossible for anyone infringing them ever to remain in society. And it was extremely difficult for any commoner, even with the advantage of great service to the country or a good marriage, to enter the charmed circle of Viennese society.

But she was at heart kindly and fair. Provided always

that there was the right sort of background men and women could count on her friendship irrespective of their wealth or brains.

From the earliest period of his career Metternich had enjoyed Countess Molly's patronage. With her numerous friends in the diplomatic world she had, when he was struggling for recognition, helped him all she could.

By then, of course, Metternich was married to Countess Eleonore, and as Countess Molly's daughter was only a baby there was no controversy over Metternich's private affairs. Indeed, the young politician's marriage to such an illustrious young woman had gained the Countess's complete approval.

But as the years went by and it became well known that Eleonore was tubercular this scheming woman began to envisage a wonderful possibility. She saw the tell-tale signs of fatal illness in the unnaturally rosy cheeks of Eleonore and she saw her own daughter Melanie emerging from adolescence to young womanhood.

When Eleonore died Countess Molly waited patiently for the end of the acceptable period of mourning before approaching Metternich directly with a proposal of marriage on her daughter's behalf. Melanie was then eighteen.

To her fury she was told of the rumours of Metternich's interest in Marie Antoinette von Leykham. Personal considerations apart, she was literally horrified that the greatest figure in the country should consider anything but an illicit liaison with a girl she considered a commoner.

'This girl is not of the Crème,' she said, using the fashionable word to describe the charmed circle of families considered to hold the exclusive right to belong to Viennese society.

The rules governing the Crème de la Crème were rigid. An Englishwoman, a Mrs. Trollope, has described an incident at a Court cotillion when the dancers were supposed to change partners. A débutante admitted to the Court ball but not to the Crème, approached a gentleman of the Crème and innocently offered him her hand for a dance.

'He looked at her in dumbfounded surprise, kept his eyes on the floor and remained motionless as if turned to stone. The blushing child turned to another, but unfortunately again she had picked a ferocious isolationist Crème de la Crème. . . .'

' "Me?" he asked with a kind of convulsive snigger, and turning on his heel began to chat with a woman of his own set who happened to be standing near him.'

Against Countess Molly's principles she issued an invitation to Marie Antoinette to attend a ball she gave so that she could check for herself if Metternich was really interested. Just one evening told her all she wanted to know, and from that moment there began the campaign of innuendo and scandal which spread through Vienna in an attempt to destroy the affair.

Thanks to Metternich's passion, she failed. For a time she avoided Metternich both at official and social affairs. The more so because he was moving heaven and earth to have his bride accepted by society—and succeeding.

Then, faced with an opposition she was for the first time in her life incapable of overcoming, Countess Molly grudgingly recognized Princess Metternich's social position by marriage and included her on her invitation list. Fortunately for both women, the meetings were few because Marie Antoinette's pregnancy occurred.

With the Princess's death in childbirth a situation which had seemed to be past redeeming was completely changed. Metternich was again a potential husband for her daughter, and Countess Molly—very much a woman of the world—saw clearly that the Chancellor was at an age when he could be strongly attracted by youth.

Melanie was then twenty-three. Her mother must have wished that she was more beautiful. She was, however, 'young and full of charm', even if she was rather plump. At her age it made her seductively attractive in a rather crude way.

The touch of the Orient in her Turkish cavalier-Hungarian ancestry had given her the most glorious ebony hair, burnished and heavy on a little head classic in shape.

What was most striking was that with such hair her eyes were of the most brilliant Aryan blue.

Some people claimed, either through admiration or envy, that her eyes were of different colour—one a pure blue and the other tinged with verdant green. This was true enough in dappled sunlight, but was a matter of sun reflection rather than a contrast in pigmentation. In one position one eye appeared green; when Melanie moved, the green hue appeared in the other.

She had, according to Madame du Montet, 'a charming face', and Mrs. Trollope wrote:

'She is young and full of charm. Her humorous and animated expression is not entirely without a touch of disdain. But that one can really pardon in a pretty young woman especially when she tempers it, as does this seductive creature, with a deliciously sweet smile that plays round her lips at the very moment of her most outrageous sallies.'

Unfortunately Melanie did not often smile. Her upbringing, spoiled and pandered to prove her high birth, yet disciplined never to be natural, had resulted in an imperiousness which had been drilled into her with some difficulty.

By nature Melanie was tempestuous and excitable, and although she had long been taught that excitement and impetuosity had to be suppressed, her temperament emerged in biting humour, often bordering on rudeness, and in bursts of temper vented on servants.

Completely dominated by her mother, she had, after Metternich's marriage to Marie Antoinette, agreed with a sigh of boredom to marry a suitor chosen by Countess Molly. He was Baron Clement von Hügel, an intelligent but simple young man whose family influence ensured him a good diplomatic post.

Beneath the cold and formal exterior of Melanie seethed considerable sexual passion. The Baron, permitted to get to know his fiancée with the chaperone discreetly occupied at the far end of the room with some embroidery, had been surprised and delighted to discover that Melanie desired much more than light conversation and an exchange of compliments.

The kisses she gave him were passionate and the way she pressed her body against him augured well for a marriage he believed was to be of pure convenience.

Despite her enormous family wealth, Melanie was avaricious and constantly demanded presents as proof of his ardour. Von Hügel was wealthy himself, but he spent more than he could afford on these gifts, learning from experience that only the very best of jewellery, bought at the most fashionable of jeweller's, would be acceptable.

Duty took him away to Paris, where he received a constant stream of enquiries about items in the Paris shops—hints which he wisely took as disguised requests, and he duly bought more gifts. He was there when Countess Molly formally informed him of the date of the wedding—almost a year hence—and this notification arrived only a week or so before the death of Marie Antoinette was announced.

When von Hügel's tour of duty was finished and he returned to Vienna he came loaded with presents, including those for the bride and bridesmaids on his wedding day. The unfortunate man had hardly entered his house when a friend, duly briefed by Countess Molly, came in to retail the latest Viennese gossip.

Prominent in the news was the report that within the week Prince Metternich was expected to announce his engagement to Countess Melanie Zichy-Ferraris.

Von Hügel was deeply upset, sufficiently so to take to his bed. But it never occurred to him to question Countess Molly, nor to tax Melanie with perfidy. He accepted the insult of an engagement broken without his knowledge and went away into self-imposed exile, saying that he would not return until he was cured of his love.

Melanie, told of this, said almost sadly:

'In that case he'll never return!'

In fact he did, and became a close friend of both Metternich and Melanie—and their devoted slave.

In the years ahead he went with the Metternichs on

most of their journeys. In fact, Count Greppi reported: 'Melanie's eyes, generally so haughty, became gentle whenever she turned them towards the man who was never far from her side.'

The day after Metternich's marriage to Melanie, with much pomp and expense, the Emperor Francis I said to her:

'Make him happy, he deserves it.'

Melanie had already decided to do just that. Soon after the honeymoon she wrote:

'I breakfasted alone today with Clement for the first time since my marriage—I was astounded at my excessive ignorance.'

She was delighted to be married and she revelled in her exalted state. She soon eclipsed even her mother's power and influence over the social life of Viennese society. She would recognize no person she did not consider of high rank and birth, but even these people could not be certain of her approval.

The basically tempestuous character made her wayward in her likes and dislikes with the result that some unfortunate person, on being introduced, would say something, or even be wearing something, which annoyed her.

From then on the victim of Melanie's dislike could not hope for further introductions either to the Metternich household or, if they were wise, to the homes of any of her friends.

Often her behaviour was outrageous. Shortly before the annual carnival of 1835 Metternich took the unusual step —for him—of agreeing with the Court authorities and the municipal governor that the tension among the people might be lessened if a great ball was held to which citizenship of Vienna would be the sole criterion of entry.

In fact, of course, the cost of admission and the necessity for expensive costumes precluded any but wealthy merchants and highly successful professional men attending. Such persons could reasonably be relied on not to exploit a situation where they were present in the same hall as the aristocracy.

Because the idea had the approval of the Chancellor everybody was agreeable—everybody, that is, except Melanie. She was furious when she heard of the scheme and ordered Metternich to have nothing to do with it. When he gently insisted on formally giving the ball his personal approval she tried blandishments to persuade him to find an excuse why he should not himself attend.

Metternich remained unusually obstinate and the arrangements went ahead. But Melanie's disgust was so strong that, for the sake of avoiding a scene in public on the night, Metternich agreed with her ultimatum that if she had to attend she would not be exposed to actual contact with the common people.

Part of the hall was roped off with crimson cords, and entry to this area was restricted to the nobility.

Many of the guests on the other side of the ropes were tradesmen—jewellers, provision merchants and furniture-makers—with whom Melanie dealt. She had practical reasons not to wish to have any conversation with them. Most were her creditors for large sums which had been outstanding for months.

The bills went unpaid not because she had no money, for Metternich's income was by this time enormous and she herself had vast resources which he had not demanded should be transferred to him in the marriage settlement.

Nor were these unfortunate creditors left in serious financial straits because she was irresponsible with money. She was, in fact, mercenary to a high degree, calculating the cost of jewellery and dresses worn by her women friends to an exactitude which was useful when she imperiously quoted the price to an obsequious tradesman that she was prepared to pay for something similar—but better.

It was just that she considered her position was dignified if she kept suppliers in their place by ignoring their bills. She took much the same attitude to the household servants, treating them harshly and, in some cases, with brutality.

The power of money fascinated her as much as the

influence of birth. Intelligent as she was, she could not judge a person's worth except in monetary values.

The young Franz Liszt was at the zenith of his fame as a pianist in the early years of Melanie's marriage. No evening entertainment was complete without him, and he could, if he had wanted, have commanded large fees. Liszt accepted an invitation from Metternich to play at his house with pleasure because he knew that the Chancellor was a genuinely cultured man and had good musical taste.

Melanie, for all her education and intelligence, was unable to discriminate between one performer and another. She judged by reputation rather than by performance.

As Liszt sat down to play she continued, as she invariably did at such entertainments, to converse with her friends. To her annoyance she got no answer and looking round the room she saw that everyone was entranced by the music.

When the applause after half an hour's playing had died away Melanie walked across and tapped the musician on the shoulder with her fan.

'You must make a lot of money, Monsieur!' she said in her high, clear voice.

Liszt stood up and bowed.

'No, Madame,' he replied, 'I make music.'

Only a genius like Liszt could have dared to make such a retort—a genius or a completely unworldly man.

There was such a man who came from Italy. Labusi had done historic work in excavating and dating Roman remains, till that time largely neglected or destroyed for the materials in them. Metternich, with his deep regard for history, was fascinated by the stories of a past Empire and was delighted when Labusi accepted an invitation to visit Vienna as his guest.

The Italian was completely wrapped up in the past and often behaved in the traditional manner of an absent-minded professor. He was unwise enough to proceed from the room Metternich had placed at his disposal to pay his respects to his hostess without gloves.

Melanie was 'sitting in state', as was her usual custom

for such occasions, on a sofa. As soon as Labusi was announced and he had bowed to her she stared back at him without speaking. Then she whispered to a footman standing behind her. The man hurried away and presently reappeared beside the visitor. On a silver salver he presented a pair of gloves.

Labusi, as proud as any Italian can be, flushed momentarily but remained 'completely master of the situation'. He took the gloves, slowly withdrew his purse, opened it, and calmly placed on the salver three pieces of silver.

Despite such superficial blemishes, the marriage, a spring and winter union of the kind which often arouses either amusement or contempt, turned out remarkably well.

Melanie, it was whispered, had always been attracted to Metternich and her heart had been almost broken when he had married Marie Antoinette von Leykham. But now Metternich was hers and proved to be as passionate and devoted in his middle fifties as even the most highly sexed wife could desire.

The frequency with which they retired early to bed even when there were guests alarmed Metternich's devoted friend Dr. Jäger, who felt it to be his duty to warn his patient that such indulgence could be physically dangerous.

Metternich, who normally kept his emotions under rigid control, burst into laughter at this, and clapped the doctor on the back with the assurance that so far from his new marriage debilitating him it was a tonic.

'You'll soon realize that I'm young in body whatever my years,' he said. 'The Princess will be consulting you.'

It was true enough. Melanie was pregnant. In five years she bore five children, and though three of them died shortly after birth, it was not any paternal defect which caused their deaths.

Metternich had found happiness again.

'I only met Melanie late in life,' he confided to a friend, 'but now I could not do without her.'

But the march of events continued to shock him to the

depths of his soul. He was on holiday beside the beautiful lake of Konigsee, not far from Salzburg, in the autumn of 1830 when a courier brought news of revolution in France, with the Bourbon Charles X abdicating in favour of Louis Phillippe.

He read the brief communication and let the paper fall from his hand. Slowly he bowed his head until it rested on his desk and he began to weep silently. Servants dared not approach him and they sent word to Melanie.

She rushed into the room and knelt beside him, fondling his hand and kissing his hair.

'All my life's work has been destroyed,' he whispered to her.

Just as she was always near her husband to comfort, reassure and influence, she personally presided over her household like a Queen. The suite where she received guests was as magnificent as that of her husband's, and there was, needless to say, an ante-chamber where guests were kept waiting, the duration being carefully calculated according to their importance—or the lack of it.

She took precedence over sixty other Princesses and never forgot to let them know it.

'I have often seen Madame de Metternich sitting alone in the middle of the drawing room for most of the evening,' M. de Sainte-Aulaire wrote. 'Other "mere mortals" were placed in armchairs too far removed to allow her to talk to them.'

Melanie gave dinner parties once or twice a week, usually intimate affairs for not more than a dozen people. In the season the great day was Sunday evening, when the Metternich ball was the accepted entertainment for every member of the nobility from the Emperor downwards.

No other hostess would have dared to organize a Sunday-evening entertainment when the Chatelaine of the Kaunitz Palace was entertaining.

The Metternichs lived there through each winter and early spring. When it became warm they would move to the villa of Rennweg which Metternich had built for himself during the Congress of Vienna.

Now that he was getting old he loved the peace of this place, fondly believing that he was living the simple life in a villa surrounded by flowers. In fact the place was full of vast salons each of which was crammed with artistic treasures and the gardens were as formal and as expensively laid out as a modest-sized Versailles.

'I wouldn't exchange my pavilion of the Rennweg,' Metternich said, 'and its present contents for all the treasures of the world.'

The Metternichs rarely remained more than a month or six weeks at Rennweg. By midsummer Melanie was accompanying her husband to Baden so that he could take the waters for his rheumatism, and she curb her constitutionally ample proportions.

Both of them implicitly believed that the spa provided a valuable source of rejuvenation, and for this reason Metternich kept rigorously to the treatment prescribed at the spa to maintain his virility.

The course of taking the waters over, they would make what amounted to a Royal progress to the estates in Bohemia and sometimes back to the Rhineland where Metternich had gone some way to restore the old glories of his own ancestral home.

Despite the ostensible holiday lasting right through the summer the routine, year after year, was exhausting for both of them. Melanie was, of course, frequently pregnant, but she still insisted that her husband should continue the social life appropriate to his rank and position.

'We had hardly got back to the house,' Melanie wrote in her diary, 'when all Vienna was upon us, the drawing room filled to overflowing.'

Metternich not only had his duties as Chancellor to carry out but the holidays were merely a replica of his social life in Vienna.

'Johannisberg is like an hotel,' Melanie reported in October 1839. 'People come here and then go off again when they have slept and eaten.'

And on another holiday she writes:

'Koenigswart Castle is so full that we couldn't take another guest and there is no more linen.'

Back home Metternich and Melanie would entertain many times a week, and on as many occasions they were guests.

There were assemblies, Court functions, fêtes, masked balls, the theatre and a dinner given by Solomon Rothschild when Melanie relates:

'He showed us his safe, unquestionably the most important piece of furniture in the house; it contains twelve millions!'

On the few days that there were no social events there were family parties attended by Metternich's children by his first marriage and, when the weather was good enough for picnics, by the nurses and the ailing babies born to Melanie.

At Christmas Metternich lit a huge Christmas tree and the children with shrieks of excitement received the innumerable toys which seemed to fill the room. Many of the most magnificent ones had been given by Baron Solomon Rothschild.

The intimate companionship of husband and wife—in an era and in a country where marriages were expected to permit each partner to live his or her own life, at least socially—was noted with amazement as well as admiration.

Melanie looked like, and of course could have been, Metternich's daughter. And the adoration patently displayed in public was not only on Metternich's side—the loving gratitude of an old man for the favours of a beautiful still-young wife. Melanie was still deeply in love with her husband. The magic which he could exert on every woman he met was still very much alive.

Although the sexual attraction for a still extraordinarily attractive man was in Melanie's case mixed with a paradoxical maternal affection for a human being who needed her care, as in everything else she did, her avaricious mind tried to dictate to her generous heart.

She may have loved Metternich for himself; she also adored him for what he was.

'I should like always to be leaning on and looking over his shoulder to see how he writes his despatches, for that is as interesting as it is curious,' she confided to her diary at the time of her marriage.

She did so. In a few years there were few occasions when Metternich conducted a conversation without Melanie being present.

When the visitor was important enough to be able to voice his distaste for the presence of a third person at delicate and off-the-record discussions she would sit hidden in an alcove with drawn curtains, a pencil and notebook in her hand. No official report arrived, and few went out, that she did not peruse.

Being intelligent, Melanie soon held as many political and diplomatic secrets as her husband.

'Clement has initiated me into his theories and projects,' she wrote in her diary. 'I have been amazed to discover the extent of my own ignorance. I want to learn to understand him at the slightest hint, to be able to help him on all occasions, to follow his discussions and to be able myself, in turn, to discuss with him; in short I want to be more than just a loving wife (which is really too easy a function).'

Being greedy and reactionary, Melanie's suggestions were invariably inimical to Metternich's real welfare and future in a world where he was gradually losing his grip and master's touch.

'I have just been with Clement for a most unusual walk through the slums,' Melanie relates on March 31st, 1843. 'A world I had never seen before; this excursion much amused us.'

Her snobbish attitude towards social class meant that Metternich was slowly cut off from intellectual advancement and first-hand knowledge of the new men who were rising to power all over Western Europe.

Writers, philosophers, demagogues, teachers and even minor but up-and-coming foreign diplomats he had once talked to simply to assess the political situation could no longer sit at his table nor even obtain an interview. The few who managed to pass the cordon Melanie erected around her husband were sycophants.

It was tragic to find this man of piercing intellect succumbing to flattery and being misled by it. The fault was not entirely Melanie's.

'Metternich was entirely surrounded by flatterers, sincere or hypocritical as the case might be,' Varnhagen reports. 'The language of flattery was the only one used in his presence, and even visitors, little accustomed to this sycophancy, soon acquired the habits of the place; they found it was the only way to get on at all.'

Metternich himself had staffed his Chancellery, and every Government department where he could exert influence, with men whose outlook coincided with his.

'With amazing efficiency,' Varnhagen says, 'the Chancellor had known how to choose his instruments: a whole gallery of living Metternichians, men permanently committed to all his ideas.'

This was not particularly dangerous while Metternich held the reins of government tightly in his own hands. But both increasing age and the demands of the social life Melanie insisted on had resulted in more and more unsupervised work being left to his underlings.

They carried out the Metternich policies of ten, twenty, even thirty years before. There was not even that slight flexibility which had enabled Metternich himself to evade failure and wrest success from imminent disaster.

But no one visualized disaster. Metternich's popularity was unequalled.

'Everywhere and on all occasions, and whatever the social class involved, conversation always got back to the Chancellor.'

He was treated like a crowned head and greeted with cannon salvos. He was recognized as a leader—and, for that matter, a superior—by all the statesmen of Europe.

'I have become the confidante of the most diverse collection of men and parties,' Metternich wrote to a friend.

'Sometimes I play the role of confessor, sometimes that of family doctor. That is why I am perhaps more the King of Prussia's Minister than Count Bernstorff; that is how I manage to keep the King of Bavaria from the brink of calamity; why Casimir Périer opens his heart to me about the dangers of his present position, and why the Pope begs me to manage his affairs.'

But time was Metternich's enemy. It took from him his most loyal friend and mentor, the Emperor. Francis died in March 1835. On his death-bed he virtually committed his Empire into the hands of his beloved Chancellor.

'Continue towards Prince Metternich, that most faithful servant and friend, the trust I have had in him for so many years. Make no decision on affairs of state and no final judgment on persons before consulting him.'

These were the words of his son Ferdinand, but, in view of the circumstances, a command to his Minister.

Ferdinand, a kind and joyful soul, was in fact mentally subnormal, an epileptic, and his face had such a bovine expression that no uniform nor palace setting could make him look even remotely regal.

The decline of Metternich, of the Austrian monarchy, and of the empire which was to be completed by 1918, had begun.

Twelve

If Metternich had been twenty years younger the existence of a semi-moron on the throne would not have greatly mattered. Metternich could have been the power behind the regal puppet.

But he was ageing, and the world was ageing too. Francis had, on the whole, been an excellent monarch.

Relying on Metternich to conduct his foreign policy, the old Emperor had nevertheless kept the supreme control in his own hands.

Possibly because he was all too aware of his son Ferdinand's disabilities, he had created a machine which ran the Government almost automatically. But, like all machines, it was not adaptable and, like many machines, it was close to being a Frankenstein monster which could not be controlled effectively.

Thus the death of one monarch and the arrival of another at first caused little upheaval. Austria progressed on her accustomed path—or, rather, she continued to slumber. But in reality there was no time to forget the troublous present and pin optimistic hopes on a brighter future. The monarch who was to bring some semblance of the greatness of Charlemagne to a so-called Empire— Franz Josef—was still a child of five.

To run Austria, a Council of State was created consisting of Metternich; the late Emperor's brother the Archduke Louis, the father of Franz Josef; and Metternich's most serious political rival, Count Kolowrat.

Encouraged by Melanie, Metternich developed his personal espionage and counter-espionage organization so that he knew everything that was going on in the country. Letters to and from the Royal Household were opened, as was diplomatic correspondence.

By making the Austrian postal service one of the best in the world Metternich ensured that foreign mail among European nations, and even between the New World and Asia, passed through Austrian territory. Anything with monogrammed seals or an address suggesting political interest was delayed for a few hours for efficient examination in what came to be known as 'Metternich's Dark Room'.

Metternich's youthful interest in chemistry aided him in suggesting fluids which would dissolve adhesives and remove seals without leaving any trace of tampering. More than eighty-five codes used by the foreign services of the world were deciphered in Vienna.

Ingenious use of lamps whose beams were intensified by lenses and mirrors enabled Metternich, whose eyesight was poor, to read documents, the covers of which defeated his chemists' attempts to open.

Melanie's insistence that the hundreds of servants they employed at their various residences should wear a distinctive livery came in very useful to disguise the chemists and deciphering experts who accompanied Metternich and his wife everywhere.

They were ready at an instant to decode a ciphered message filched from a French diplomatic bag or to amuse Melanie by opening a love-letter sent to some Duchess.

Periodically Metternich suffered from a slight physical collapse which suggested a heart attack. Some of the social glory of the Metternich household declined due to the enforced quietness, but even so Melanie rarely omitted to hold at least two evening receptions every week.

Metternich knew, naturally, that as he approached his seventies active political life, with a daily routine usually occupying him for fifteen hours, would slow down.

In preparation for retirement he built a magnificent mansion within sight of his Rennweg villa. He was, in fact, perfectly content with the villa and its gardens, but Melanie had no intention of living modestly when the official residence of the Chancellor would no longer be theirs. It was she who insisted that they must have a home comparable with their social status. The house was completed in 1847.

By then it was not the burden of the years which made a place of refuge necessary but the impact of events. Revolutions and *coups d'état* were occurring all over Europe. Austria's provinces in Italy were to all intents and purposes in successful revolt. Hungary, that junior partner in the Empire, was demanding equality if not independence. Bohemia was breeding the type of Czech who was to become a byword as a fighter for freedom.

Metternich chose to ignore the signs—or at least to laugh them off.

'Metternich's imperturbability alarms me,' wrote Baron

Hübner. 'I wonder what they would do should the worst happen? Metternich stands alone and he seems paralysed and powerless.'

It was not until the spring of the ominous year 1848 that Metternich saw the end of his career was very near.

On February 28th Anselm de Rothschild brought him the news that France had been declared a Republic. He collapsed on the verge of fainting into his armchair.

'Well, my friend, it's all up now!' he exclaimed later when the Russian Chargé d'Affaires brought him the same information.

'The judgments of God are terrible!' Melanie moaned.

Metternich forced himself to recover sufficiently to preside over the evening's reception which followed a Cabinet meeting. He sat receiving his guests with an air of such serenity that even the foreign diplomats were impressed and believed that the old man had something up his sleeve.

In actual fact he was exerting an iron control over his physical weakness, hardly daring to move or speak in case he betrayed his real condition.

The Prussian Minister wrote of this party:

'Last night there were a great many people in Prince Metternich's drawing room, chiefly diplomatists. . . . The impression produced here by the recent events in Paris is formidable . . .'

All the Ambassadors were in an obvious state of agitation.

'I have never lived through such an evening,' wrote Baron Hübner.

The next day Vienna was in an uproar. Within a fortnight it was not only the Viennese mob who were cursing the name of Metternich. The Court sycophants, seeing the danger signals and anxious to find a culprit, began to intrigue against Metternich.

'Revolutions spread quickly,' he remarked and he wrote to Kaunitz saying:

'In the last analysis I prefer the worst to the merely bad: it is more clear-cut. I feel calmer than before the struggle began. I am standing firm. Nothing can baffle me.'

Melanie took refuge in prayer.

'We are all very anxious at Court,' she wrote in her diary. 'Today they all look to my poor Clement for help; they also wish to make him responsible for the errors of others in the past.'

Metternich, so fixed in his ideas, so certain that his 'Dark Room' and his police would reveal every secret move towards revolution, continued calm and assured.

Neither his agents nor he seemed to realize that an unaccountably large stream of invoices and orders for candles going through the post presaged something special —and disastrous.

The City of Waltzes conducted its revolution in its own inimitable manner. Students and shopkeepers marched singing through the streets, pausing outside the Hofburg to cheer their Emperor, who appeared at a window and drooled a smile of pleasure.

It was only when the crowd swarmed into the Bullhausplatz that the shouts became hostile. The name of Metternich was on every lip, and it was pronounced like a curse. Metternich stood at the window, trying to grasp what was being said.

A medical student shouted:

'The road to liberty is open . . . if Austria still hangs back she owes it more than anything to a faulty system of education. But it is not the Emperor we have to blame . . . only that unpopular Minister who is at the head of the Government—Prince Metternich! But his days are numbered, and when Nature has run her course, we shall be free!'

Metternich banged his fist on the table.

'The sickness has come to the surface at last,' he cried.

By the afternoon firing had broken out and a score of demonstrators were casualties. It was then that Metternich, dressed elegantly in his green tail-coat with light grey trousers, went to confer with the Archduke Franz Charles who, he knew, was both responsible for the activities of the trigger-happy troops and the intrigues against himself.

Metternich insisted that giving way to the demands of the mob would be fatal. He wanted forceful but restrained measures to restore order.

'When I think of all the imbecilities I heard in the course of that famous thirteenth of March,' he said later, 'I often ask myself whether those people were mad or merely drunk.'

His colleagues were so frightened about the situation and so hostile to Metternich that no decision was made. Metternich returned to his house and walked in the exceptionally balmy March evening with Melanie. He could hear the crowd shouting outside the walls which surrounded his estate. By the time darkness fell, the Government, in the person of Archduke Louis, was demanding Metternich's resignation.

'I submit to a power superior to that of my Emperor himself,' Metternich said as he wrote out his resignation.

The Archdukes and Ministers tried to thank him for making things easier for them, but Metternich waved them aside.

'I am making no sacrifice, merely doing my duty,' he said, and left the Hofburg.

He looked around at the frightened men who had fawned on him for years.

'I shall not be taking the monarchy with me,' he added sarcastically. 'No one has broad enough shoulders to do that. Monarchies disappear when they lose confidence in themselves.'

Melanie, suffering from a feverish cold, was waiting for him at home. She put her arm around his shoulders, bent and frail in this moment of political death.

'Have we all been murdered?' she asked.

'Yes, my dear,' he replied. 'We have all been murdered.'

They went into their private suite, shutting out the world they no longer understood.

'I thank God,' Metternich said when they were alone, 'I have been allowed to remain detached from current events;

the overthrow of the existing social order is now inevitable. I could not have avoided concessions which will inevitably lead to chaos. As things are, I am saved the shame of signing them.'

Melanie wrote all he said in her diary, adding:

'Clement was resigned, calm and almost happy.'

They prepared for bed early. From the darkened room they could see beyond the great windows Vienna illuminated. Thousands upon thousands of candles burned in the windows of the houses, even in the poverty-stricken slums which Melanie had once visited and found 'so amusing'. The people were celebrating the downfall of Metternich.

Next morning the authorities sent a platoon of soldiers to guard the ex-Chancellor. They were there to ensure protection until the Metternichs could flee the city.

A handful of friends came to offer help and pay respects, but the men whose careers existed thanks to Metternich, and the women who had moved heaven and earth to ingratiate themselves with Melanie, kept studiously away.

Melanie, whose life had been spent in arrogance, now showed her real love for her husband by her unremitting comfort of him and a display of cheerful courage. Gone were the insistence on etiquette and the greedy lust for possessions. Her only preoccupation was for Metternich's welfare and, indeed, his life.

Late that night, in an ordinary cab driven by the brother of Melanie's first fiancé, and Metternich's loyal friend, Clement von Hügel, they began their journey to exile.

The Mayor of Feldsberg refused to permit them to rest in the town; the Archbishop of Olmutz forbade them to enter his diocese; at the railway stations mobs quickly gathered to jeer at the old man who, whatever his errors in his old age, had saved their fathers and themselves from the death and desolation of war.

Passing quickly through Germany, not daring to stop elsewhere in Europe, the Metternichs arrived in London and stayed at the Mirvat Hotel, on the site of the present Claridges. Finance was a problem for a couple who had not known for a lifetime what it was to worry for a second about sources of almost unlimited income.

Metternich's estates in Bohemia and Austria, as well as their Viennese possessions and banking accounts, were frozen on the pretext of misappropriation of State funds—a charge eventually to be withdrawn as baseless.

With an amazing display of optimism, vitality, pride and courage, Metternich smiled at his misfortunes and his exile.

'Placed as I am now, from an observatory with a worldwide horizon,' he said on March 28th, 1848, 'I have no reason to complain of my personal fate. It is the world I pity.'

After a few months Metternich rented a house at 44 Eaton Square in Belgravia and a semblance of the old glory returned as all London society showed their contempt for the revolutionary trends abroad in London by fêting the arch-figure of reaction.

In the streets people recognized and cheered him.

'We could not have been better received in London,' he said, 'had I been John Bull in person.'

Despite the practical help of English friends, notably the Duke of Wellington who called every morning, and Metternich's old political adversary, Lord Palmerston, money problems forced the Metternichs to return to Europe. They rented a house in Brussels.

Three years of virtual homelessness ended when, in June 1851, they entered their old home at Johannisberg on the banks of the Rhine.

'The Rhine runs in my veins,' Metternich exclaimed, 'and the sight of it enchants me!'

The house was magnificent. It had once been an abbey and had been the gift of the Emperor Francis shortly after his Coronation. Later it had become one of the most famous of all Rhenish wine centres.

But Metternich's eyes were fixed on Vienna, his true home despite his love of the Rhineland. Ferdinand I had abdicated in December 1848. Young Franz Josef, steeped in the ideologies which Metternich had taught him from childhood, was now on the throne of the Empire, and the heady excitement of liberalism engendered by the revolution seemed to have been consigned to oblivion. The old regime was once again in favour with the rulers and seemingly with the ruled.

In the summer of 1851 the Metternichs were back in the Austrian capital. Despite the stabilization of government, this was not the Vienna they had known. Metternich was treated courteously but not permitted to contribute to the councils of the statesmen.

But Viennese society welcomed them with open arms.

'In the first days after our arrival,' Melanie recorded in her diary, 'we were so swamped with callers, it would be impossible to count them.'

Melanie was soon complaining at the sort of people she found were fellow guests at entertainments and receptions to which she was invited.

'They had invited all the wrong people,' she wrote, 'those we used to consider "the second society", circles whose leading ladies are much too flamboyantly smart. One saw no sign of mixing with the cream.'

Metternich was at an age when small things no longer irritated him. He was reconciled to his new position and even to the new Vienna.

'He no longer either felt bitterness or any desire for revenge,' the Duke Ernest of Coburg related.

Memories of the bygone years when love had been so violently a part of his life were constantly revived in almost grotesque vividness. Princess Lieven had been in London when they were there and had become a 'character'. She wore black on every occasion and hid her raddled and powdered face under an immense hat with a green veil. She always carried a huge fan.

Metternich's grand-daughter, the Princess Pauline, poked fun at her.

'Solemn and impressive,' she wrote, 'she would pass without deigning to look on us poor worms!'

The two old lovers met and neither found the other very attractive. Metternich saw an old harridan still attempting to be the grand lady. Dorothea found her one-time lover 'fatuous, very slow, very heavy, very dull, obscure and boring when his subject was himself and his infallibility'.

But Dorothea was spiteful and jealous of Melanie, whom she thought fat and vulgar, and she wouldn't admit, even to herself, how brilliant Metternich still was.

The young Disraeli started a close friendship with the ex-Chancellor, and years later, when lengthy correspondence had been exchanged, he found Metternich's letters 'so full of ideas that they will never grow old'.

In London, in Brussels where Metternich had stayed for a time on his journey from London to Johannisberg, and in Vienna, more ghosts of his past loves emerged.

The Duchesse de Sagan had worn remarkably well. She still dressed beautifully, looked distinguished, and her intelligence and wit were unimpaired. But her name and her reputation counted for little. Like Metternich, she had to live on glories of the past—glories too many people of the day had never known about.

Most frightening of all was Katharina Bagration. Intimidated by the implications of age, she had retreated both mentally and physically into the wonderful days of her youth when her beauty and charm could ensnare any man her master, the long-dead Tsar, had named.

Constant bleaching of her grey hair in order to retrieve the blonde curls of her girlhood had made her almost bald. Horror of fatness had resulted in her following a starvation diet which reduced her body to a living skeleton on which the flesh hung in withered folds. She wore hats and dresses suitable only for a teen-age girl of fifty years earlier.

Her yellowed parchment skin could be seen through diaphanous sleeves and above her low *décolletage*. Her claw-like fingers were embellished with gaudy rings. She liked to fix roses round her head to disguise the lack of hair.

Though they lived on for a few years more, Metternich

had no wish to see such spectres. He was entirely wrapped up in Melanie, his prop and shield, and his constant companion every hour of the day and night. He became uneasy if she left his presence even for a few minutes.

Melanie died after a serious illness in March 1854. Metternich sat at her bedside and watched her life ebb gently away. At the end the woman who had so faithfully mothered him for twenty-two years slipped her hand, like a little child seeking security and comfort, into his.

'Her last moments,' he wrote, 'might be compared with a light going slowly out.'

Metternich lived on for five years, until he was eighty-six. All his mental faculties were still active.

'I am dead,' he said with a smile, 'but I belong to that category of corpses in which the nerves are still vibrating and who can still be galvanized by issues affecting principle.'

By then all the women he had loved were dead and gone—their tombs merely a record of a name, a birth date and an ending.

They, like their lover, had belonged to another age. Their like will not be seen again; nor will there be a statesman of world renown who openly, but with such extreme elegance, 'lived in sin'.

The loves of Fürst von Clement Wenceslas Nepomuk Lothar Metternich, within the marital state or beyond it, softened the character of someone whose icy intellect produced a figure of superhuman coldness, objectivity and brilliance.

In the consideration of his times and his country he was a great statesman. Thanks to the fervour of his love and passion for the women who adored him over a period of nearly half a century it is also right to say: here was a Man!

Bibliography

British History of the Nineteenth Century:
G. M. Trevelyan
Congress of Vienna, The: C. K. Webster
Diplomates Romantiques: M. Paleologue
François II, la Beau-père de Napoleon: Von Bibl
Fürst Metternich: K. Groos
Hapsburg Monarchy, The: A. J. P. Taylor
History of Mediaeval Austria: A. W. A. Leeper
Holy Alliance, The: W. P. Cresson
Holy Roman Empire, The: H. A. L. Fisher
Josephine, Empress of France: Barbara Cartland
L'Imperatrice Marie Louise: M. Masson
Lettres du Prince Metternich à la Princesse de Lieven:
J. Hanotaux
Life of Metternich: A. Cecil
Life of Prince Metternich: D. G. Malleson
Maria Theresa: K. Tschuppik
Mediaeval Empire, The: H. A. L. Fisher
Memoires: Comte de Bray
*Memoires du Prince de Talleyrand; Memoires inédits de
M. de Metternich:* C. de Grunwald
Memoires: Metternich
Metternich: A. Cecil
Metternich: C. de Grunwald
Metternich: S. von Rabensberg
Metternich: Andre Robert
Metternich: C. A. Sandeman
Metternich: F. B. Schaefer

Napoleon the Man: R. McNair Wilson
Prince Metternich in Love and War: de Reichenburg
Private Letters of Princess Lieven: Edited by P. Quennell
Three Studies in European Conservatism: E. L. Woodward
Viennese Court and State Archives

THE END

DIANE DE POITIERS by BARBARA CARTLAND

When Diane de Poitiers was born to joyful parents in the little town of Saint-Vallier, in the valley of the Rhone, an old crone prophesied 'she will cause tears to fall and joys to be known. And those who weep and those who rejoice she will be greater than them all.' Diane was indeed destined to be great – she was a descendant of Louis XI and related by marriage to Charles VII. As she grew up she displayed formidable qualities of intelligence – and her beauty was just as remarkable. When her lover, Henri, was crowned King, she skilfully piloted him through the first difficult months of his reign. She was an important member of the King's Privy Council, controlling its members as well as its master.

Barbara Cartland's biography of Diane de Poitiers is a glowing tale of the achievements of the King's mistress. Today she and Henri are still remembered for their unchanging, indivisible and eternal love ...

0 552 10065 X – 40p

THE SCANDALOUS LIFE OF KING CAROL by BARBARA CARTLAND

KING CAROL OF ROUMANIA – Heir to a stormy and tempestuous throne – he was to suffer all his life from the actions brought about by his violent, passionate nature. From his first poignant affair during World War I, to the vibrant heady passion for Madame Lupescu, Carol was to scandalise the capitals of the world with his unrestrained emotions ...

Barbara Cartland, novelist, playwright, lecturer, T.V. personality and President of the National Association for Health, recounts the incredible story of a King who was prepared to risk his throne in the cause of love.

0 552 09535 4 – 35p

THE GOLDEN BEES by THEO ARONSON

'Theo Aronson accomplishes pleasantly and with great skill his difficult task of taking the Bonaparte family from its Corsican years to the present day.' – *Daily Telegraph*

'The canvas is dramatically large, and he has filled it well. He has marshalled armies of fact, and reviewed them in excellent order . . . a competent, highly coloured, readable popular survey.' – *Punch*

'An excellent study of the Bonapartes.' – *Sunday Express*

0 552 09704 – 95p

OLIVER CROMWELL by C. V. WEDGWOOD

Has been described as an honest, independent gentleman farmer, subject to fits of melancholy; a Puritan convert, burning with religious zeal; a reluctant dictator; and a brilliant soldier-statesman who put an end to civil war, restored peace at home and respect abroad.

He was over forty before his genius as a soldier was revealed – a genius which combined with his political skills to bring him within reach of the Crown. In this brilliantly concentrated biography, Dame Veronica Wedgwood explores the policies and character of the man who, as Lord Protector of Great Britain and Ireland, enjoyed supreme power for five years and still remained an enigma both to his contemporaries and to students of history today.

'The essence of Cromwell's career in a nutshell – brisk, reliable, brief.' – *Sunday Telegraph*

'. . . a miracle of concentrated historical writing . . . This book has all the virtues: objectivity, clarity of interpretation, brevity and genuine historical insight.'
– *Books and Bookmen*

0 552 09881 7 – 50p

A SELECTED LIST OF CORGI AUTOBIOGRAPHIES AND BIOGRAPHIES FOR FOR YOUR READING PLEASURE

☐ 09393 9	THE KAISERS (illus.)	Theo Aronson	80p
☐ 09704 7	THE GOLDEN BEES	Theo Aronson	95p
☐ 99451 0	CLEOPATRA (Illus.)	Ernle Bradford	80p
☐ 09373 6	OUR KATE	Catherine Cookson	35p
☐ 09557 5	DEVIL'S BLOOD	Alfred Duggan	50p
☐ 09067 0	LOUIS XIV (Illus.)	Philippe Erlanger	90p
☐ 09269 X	NERO (Illus.)	Michael Grant	80p
☐ 07400 4	MY LIFE AND LOVES	Frank Harris	95p
☐ 09066 2	CHARLES I (Illus.)	Christopher Hibbert	75p
☐ 09153 7	THE TSARS	Ronald Hingley	70p
☐ 09230 4	BUGLES AND A TIGER	John Masters	40p
☐ 09330 0	THE PILGRIM SON	John Masters	40p
☐ 09065 4	CATHERINE THE GREAT (Illus.)	Zoe Oldenbourg	80p
☐ 09783 7	THE LIFE AND DEATH OF ADOLF HITLER	Robert Payne	£1.25
☐ 68070 2	CONFESSIONS OF A HOPE FIEND	Timothy Leary	50p
☐ 09449 8	GREY MISTRESS	Joy Packer	50p
☐ 09450 1	APES AND IVORY	Joy Packer	50p
☐ 09448 X	PACK AND FOLLOW	Joy Packer	50p
☐ 09881 7	OLIVER CROMWELL	C. V. Wedgwood	60p

All these books are available at your bookshop or newsagent; or can be ordered direct from the publisher. Just tick the titles you want and fill in the form below.

CORGI BOOKS, Cash Sales Department, P.O. Box 11, Falmouth, Cornwall.

Please send cheque or postal order, no currency. **U.K. and Eire** send 15p for first book plus 5p per copy for each additional book ordered to a maximum charge of 50p to cover the cost of postage and packing. **Overseas Customers and B.F.P.O.** allow 20p for first book and 10p per copy for each additional book.

NAME (block letters)..

ADDRESS ....

(JAN. 76) ....

While every effort is made to keep prices low, it is sometimes necessary to increase prices at short notice. Corgi Books reserve the right to show new retail prices on covers which may differ from those previously advertised in the text or elsewhere.